Guilty as Blood

Guilty as
BLOOD

One Can Make a Difference

R. C. Jette

RESOURCE *Publications* · Eugene, Oregon

GUILTY AS BLOOD
One Can Make a Difference

Resource Publications
An Imprint of Wipf and Stock Publishers
199 W. 8th Ave., Suite 3
Eugene, OR 97401

www.wipfandstock.com

PAPERBACK ISBN: 978-1-7252-5826-6
HARDCOVER ISBN: 978-1-7252-5827-3
EBOOK ISBN: 978-1-7252-5828-0

Manufactured in the U.S.A.   DECEMBER 2, 2019

This book is dedicated to my Lord Jesus Christ, to my husband, Paul, who has been by my side through thick and thin, to my son (PJ) his daughter (Keira), to my daughter (Dawn), to my daughter (Christina) her sons (Andrew, Matthew, Joshua) and her daughter (Sarah who is with the Lord), to Susanna and Mike who have been such a help, and to all who have influenced my life throughout the years.

Special thanks is given to Wipf and Stock Publishers for their amazing help that has been such a godsend to me.

Very special thanks is given to Matthew Wimer, Daniel Lanning, George Callihan, and Shannon Carter who through their understanding have helped encourage me to keep on writing.

Previously published through Resource Publications:

Nonfiction:

1. *Storms Are Faith's Workout: Preparing Christians for Spiritual Ambush (2018).*

2. *Faith's Journey Confronts Obstacles: Instructing God's Soldiers to Overcome in His Armor (2019).*

3. *Satan's Strategy to Torment Through Physical Ambush: Educating God's Soldiers of Satan's Plot to Shatter Faith Through Sickness and Disease (2019).*

4. *Spiritual Shipwreck on the Horizon: Exhorting Christians to Contend for the Faith and Comprehend the Deceitfulness of Sin (2019).*

5. *Satan Has no Authority Over God's Soldier: Illuminating Godlike Faith (2019).*

6. *God: The Holy Spirit: The Conquering Power Within (2019).*

Fiction:

1. *The Elfdins and the Gold Temple: An Oralee Chronicle (2018).*

2. *Charlie McGee and the Leprechaun: Life's Curious Twist of Events (2019).*

3. *The Shrines of Manitoba: Dark Secrets Shall Be Brought to Light (2019).*

SAND CASTLES

Sometimes we build our present,
Upon former and bygone dreams,
No longer possible,
For there's no future in the past.

As ocean waves wash ashore,
Earlier dreams like sand castles,
Must be washed out to sea,
Allowing us to dream anew!
—R. C. JETTE

Contents

Chapter 1

The Black Cat

"What the blazes?" Officer Luke Drake said, as he watched a red Toyota leaving a trail of burnt rubber screech to a halt several yards in front of his squad car. As the car halted, a black cat bolted out of the way. Luke let out a heavy sigh. "That dumb cat almost caused an accident." He threw up his hands. "Never mind that, it nearly lost its life."

Before he could get to the vehicle to check on the driver, it backed up and sped away. His first instinct was to pursue, but he felt it was essentially the cat's fault. He gave a heavy sigh. "No sense speeding off after the car. It's obvious she stopped quickly to avoid hitting the stupid cat and was in control of the situation." He grabbed his notebook. "I'll just jot a few notes in here. Never know if I might need the plate number."

His face screwed up. "What is it Lord, I feel strange?" He looked up at the sight of two red eyes glaring at him. There on the top of his squad car sat the black cat. "Oh, my, I do pray this isn't a warning or something." He stroked his chin with his right thumb and forefinger. "Well, I'll not be frightened by a black cat or anything else. Besides, Pastor O'Reilly preached Sunday there's no room for fear in a Christian's life." He took a deep breath and opened his car door. As the door opened, the cat meowed, jumped on the curb, and ran down an alley between two buildings.

Luke sat back in his squad car and pondered the black cat episode. "Why do I sense the cat means something?" He gazed up, when his blue eyes caught sight of the birds chirping and twittering back and forth. One would rush from one building to another, and a second would fly to a further group, all the while chirping away. As he watched the tiny amphibians for some time, he was mesmerized by their activity and gazed in amazement. "Lord, even the innocent creatures seem to be caught up in gossip. Why does it have such a hold on so many? Even those who sit in church on Sunday and Wednesday busy themselves with gossip all week. It's like tale bearing has them securely in its grip. No matter where I go outside of church, I hear gossip." He paused. "At least I can visit with Pastor O'Reilly and be free of gossipmongers." He threw up his hands. "It's so difficult when my sister seems to be the chief of gossip at her diner. Instead of it being May's Diner, it should say House of Gossip." He combed back his black curls with his right hand. "I don't know how many times Pastor O'Reilly has taught about Burroughville being big on prejudice and gossip. Aborigines were in and outsiders were out. He's tried to reveal how it displeases the Lord, but just a few heed his messages."

While Luke pondered how he could be a light to help people see they were respecter of persons, he caught sight of a black Ferrari. Elizabeth Johnson had been the center of hearsay for a couple of years after she and Barth moved into town. Local rumormongers fumed about outsiders purchasing the Vandyke Manor, the most illustrious mansion in Burroughville, and gossip worked overtime to find justification for its bias. Gossipers were elated to hear the police were called to the Johnson manor for a family disturbance.

Elizabeth was said to have a short fuse with her husband, which made no sense when he saw her gentle manner in church. Besides, Luke knew with a wife like her, he wouldn't be away so often, whether or not his business was in Capital City. But police visits to the Johnson place have ceased, and their arguments have lost the flare, not spicy enough anymore. Even his sister's place, gossip headquarters, has focused its rumors elsewhere.

Observing Main Street, Luke was dispirited with the town's enchantment with tittle-tattle. Everywhere he looked, he saw couples walking hand in hand. On duty or not, he'd still be alone. He'd dated a few of the locals, but their interest in police gossip turned him off. He tried to explain he was only interested in the truth about a situation and not hearsay or speculation. It didn't take long to figure out they were more interested in what they could hear to gossip about than in him. When he refused to talk about his job, they soon found someone else to date.

Borroughville's discrimination had always been a problem to Luke. He believed people should spend their time in something constructive and not the destructive practice of gossip. After he earned his degree in Theology, the Lord led him to go to the Police Academy. But since he joined the force about ten years ago, he'd witnessed so much prejudice he felt soiled just being in the town.

His purpose for joining, besides obedience to the Lord, was he believed God said one could make a difference in the town. The Lord impressed him that a simple spark can cause a raging fire. It was difficult at times, when he felt he was making no headway. After all, he couldn't even seem to make a difference with his own sister. Instead of backing off her hearsay, she seemed to add to her tale bearing. Gossip was May's full-time hobby.

Luke's thoughts were interrupted by a call from dispatch. He was informed about a disturbance at the Johnson Manor.

§

His heart fluttered as he drove up to the perimeter wall and pulled into the gated entrance. Driving down the long driveway, he noticed the large lawn with manicured hedges and shrubs. Once at the end of the driveway, it circled to the front entry. He took a deep breath to calm himself. "Lord, I do pray this isn't new fuel for gossip. You know what this town is like." He blew out a heavy sigh. "Well, here goes," he said as he pulled up to the entrance of the manor.

The butler hurried to the squad car before it came to a stop. With trembling hands, he opened Luke's door. "Officer," he said with a definite British accent. "I came home to get Sarah a cloak. She's my wife. I didn't want her to catch a chill. She's had the sniffles of late. But if you ask me, I'd have hit the bloke long before this. Me and the Missus don't say naught. Believe me, Miss Elizabeth has put up with much from the blaggard."

"Wait a minute!" Luke got out of the squad car. "I have no idea what you're talking about?"

"So sorry, officer, but I'm rather in a tizzy." He paused. "You know I'm Harold Simpson, Miss Elizabeth's butler." He scratched the back of his head with his right hand. "Blimey, this is most unsettling." He composed himself. "I came home, heard Miss Elizabeth scream, ran into the parlor, and saw Barth stretched out on the floor. She stood near him holding the bronze bust of Mozart that looked bloody. Barth gasped something like, 'Don't hit me again,' and then he didn't move." He caught his breath. "I figured I had better call the police straight away, and that's what I did."

"For pity's sake man, show me to the parlor."

He gestured with his right hand. "It's this way. Please follow me." He paused. "Miss Elizabeth doesn't look too good. I'm quite concerned about her. She's been through so much with the blaggard with his gambling, drinking, and always wanting more money."

Harold led him through an expansive entryway with double doors. Inside, Luke saw high ceilings with crown molding and stained-glass windows. He was breathless at the spacious rooms, chandeliers, heavy curtains, and valuable paintings adorning the walls.

He blinked and shook his head when Harold spoke. "It's through here. Miss Elizabeth is sitting over there."

Luke couldn't help himself as he looked about in wonder. He thought he was in antique paradise. Forcing himself to ignore he was sort of an enthusiast of antiques, he quickly viewed the scene.

Barth lay on his stomach, the left side of his head in a pool of blood. To Barth's left, Elizabeth, bronze bust in her hand, sat transfixed on a Hepplewhite sofa. On the floor near the front window, a small mahogany table was overturned, and near the table laid a Tiffany lamp. Although a Persian carpet seemed to soften the lamp's fall, it took great stamina for Luke not to pick up the leaded glass shade to see if there were any cracks. In a small alcove opposite the fireplace stood a parquetry commode, the embroidered runner hung by a bronze knob revealing a flawless marble top. On the oak floor was a broken lead-glazed vase, and what looked like a Gobelin tapestry lay in a pile near an empty wall. The evidence pointed to an apparent struggle of some kind.

A spasm crossed Luke's face as he headed toward the victim; it was all he could do to appear calm. He wasn't pleased with the look of things. Breathing deeply, he checked Barth for a pulse, but there was none. Next, he noticed the victim had a large clotted gash on the right side of his head. Jotting the findings in his notebook, Luke caught sight of Harold as he approached Elizabeth. He quickly stood in front to stop him before he could reach her. "You'll have to stay out of this room. It's now considered a crime scene. We have to make sure nothing is touched."

"Is he dead?" Harold muttered.

Elizabeth stood up, dropped the figurehead, and went towards Barth. Luke swiftly grabbed her arm. "Sorry, but you can't go near him. Please stay away." He gave out a heavy sigh. "I'm sorry, but this looks very serious."

She looked around dazed. "Where's Aurora?"

Harold gestured with his right hand. "You know she stays clear of the bloke." He paused. "She's probably hiding as usual. Once she knows it's safe, she'll show herself."

"I know you're not yourself," Luke said to Elizabeth, "but you'll both have to come with me. We have to move to another room. Is there a telephone handy? I need to call homicide." At Luke's question, Harold headed toward the body. "Not that one," Luke said grabbing the butler's arm. "You can't go near there. I told you it's now a crime scene, and nothing can be touched.

Luke helped Elizabeth, while Harold led them into the adjoining room. Sliding mahogany doors separated the parlor from the sitting room. Standing between the two rooms, Luke called homicide. When he finished his call, he perused his surroundings. Against the far wall of the sitting room was an ebony chest of drawers with ornate metal inlay on tortoiseshell proudly displaying a mahogany birdcage with elaborately detailed carving. On either side of a Chippendale piecrust tripod table were two Chippendale chairs with cabriole legs and claw-and-ball feet. Harold sat on the chair closest to Luke. Elizabeth, facing the fireplace, sat in a large Queen Anne chair.

§

When the detectives arrived, the coroner and Chief Hopkins were right behind. Luke could tell by the look on the chief's face he was enjoying this. Instead of the chief of police, he should've been the chief of rumormongers. Luke didn't relish relaying what he saw when arriving on the scene. Why did he have to be the one to see the weapon in Elizabeth's hand? But he knew there must be a reason for him to be there. When you serve the Lord, nothing happens by chance. God has a purpose for him to be the first one there. He was grateful to the Lord that Pastor O'Reilly had given him permission to stop by any time he needed to talk. He would need the pastor's advice before getting supper at his sister's diner tonight.

Luke no sooner finished his account of things, when the chief assumed a posture of superiority. "Okay Drake," he snickered. "We'll handle it from here. If I have any questions, I know where to reach you. Besides, I believe your shift is up, and I'm sure May will have your supper ready." He gave a smirk. "If I didn't know you two were brother and sister, I would've never figured it out. May's a real down to earth gal, whereas, you seem to be floating in the clouds most of the time with your Bible quotes."

At that moment, a tall, slender, stunning brunette, carrying a briefcase, walked in. A detective stopped her. "Who the devil are you? How did you get past the officers outside?"

"My name is Dorine Morse, and I'm Mr. Johnson's secretary. He called me and asked me to bring some important papers for him to sign. It couldn't wait until Monday." She took a drag of her cigarette and blew the smoke in the detective's direction. "If you don't mind, what business is it of yours?"

The chief interrupted, as usual, to take control. "Look, young lady, a homicide is police business, and you have no business being here. I'd advise you to mind your manners."

"Wait a minute! Dorine shrieked. "Did you say a homicide?" She dropped her briefcase. "You mean someone's dead?"

"Well, young lady, that's what a homicide means," the chief sneered.

"Who's dead?" Dorine said, nervously putting her cigarette out in a bronze bowl.

"I'm afraid your boss won't be signing any more papers." He snickered and gestured toward Luke. "Of course, unless our Officer Drake can bring the dead back to life through his Bible quotes."

"No!" Dorine cried. "He can't be dead." Her eyes scanned the room and stopped at Elizabeth. "You!" She screamed. Like a flash, she ran toward Elizabeth and grabbed her by the throat. "You money hungry witch; you killed him. I knew you'd be his death. If he'd listened to me, he'd still be alive."

Luke and the chief pulled her away from Elizabeth. "Drake!" Chief Hopkins said straightening himself into his posture of superiority. "Get her out of here before I charge her with assault."

A detective handcuffed Elizabeth, and the chief read the Miranda Rights. As Luke left, he heard Elizabeth say in a low, tormented voice, "I didn't do it. When I came home, I found him lying on the floor with the Mozart bust next to him. I didn't realize anything was wrong until I picked it up and saw the blood. I just thought he was drunk as usual."

§

Once outside, Luke took down Dorine's name and address. "In case the chief needs to speak with you, we need to have all necessary information. You do understand it's all part of police procedure?"

"I understand," Dorine wept. "I'm sorry for the spectacle in there, but I guess I lost it. He was a great boss, and she always gave him a hard time." She composed herself. "I'll be all right. It was the shock. If you'll excuse me, I think I'd better go home. I really need to get my thoughts together. It's quite bizarre to suddenly find myself unemployed."

Luke tried to focus on her words, but a bleak, wintry feeling consumed his energy. He gave her an affirmative nod and got into his squad car. After Dorine drove out of sight, Luke just sat in his car. "Lord, what am I going to do? Something tells me there's a rat here, but I don't know what to do. I do realize things are not always what they seem to be." He combed back his black curls with his right hand. "I heard what Elizabeth said, and I believe her. But I know the whole town will be rejoicing at her arrest." He paused. "Please, Lord, give me wisdom to help her prove her innocence. Only you can lead me to the truth."

Once the reporters showed up, he headed for town. He needed to talk to Pastor O'Reilly.

Chapter 2

God Knows Beginning and End

Luke couldn't thank the Lord enough for bringing Pastor O'Reilly to Burroughville Christian Fellowship Church. Although he'd only been there about five years, Pastor O'Reilly was a true man of God who helped Luke grow stronger in his faith. Apparently, the pastor's wife passed away a few years before he came to town. She was the daughter of John Myers, the previous mayor, who was well liked by all. Luke believed it was to please Mr. Myers the church voted Pastor O'Reilly in. However, he wasn't sure how many wished they hadn't. He'd noticed many with ear plugs in their ears during service. There's not too many wanting to hear the sermons coming from Pastor O'Reilly. It's obvious they wished for a preacher with itching ears in the pulpit to pamper their flesh.

As Luke pulled up to the parsonage, he saw lights on, and was relieved the pastor was still up. He hurried to the front door and rang the doorbell.

When Pastor O'Reilly opened the door, he clasped his hands. "Why, Luke, how nice to see you." He motioned with his right hand. "Won't you come in?"

"I won't keep you long, but I'm disturbed about a matter."

"If you're troubled about something, I know it's important. I just made myself a pot of chamomile tea. You can tell me what's on your mind over a cup." He led Luke into the kitchen. "Have a seat, while I get another cup." He poured them both a cup of tea and sat on the chair across from Luke. "Now, what's your concern?"

"I was called out to the Johnson Manor tonight about a disturbance. When I arrived, the butler met me outside. He rattled on about something I didn't understand." He took a sip of his tea. "Anyway, it seems Barth Johnson is dead. When I entered the parlor, Elizabeth had the murder weapon in her hand."

"Oh my! I find it hard to believe Elizabeth is capable of such a thing. We've had many conversations." He rubbed the back of his neck with his right hand. "Unless, she says I can say anything, I can't divulge our talks. I will say she's a true woman of God who found herself in an unpleasant situation because of lies and deceit, but she is faithful to the Lord."

"I understand about confidentiality. As I was leaving the room, they handcuffed her. I heard her whisper she didn't do it and thought he was drunk as usual. She didn't realize anything was amiss until she picked up the Mozart bust and saw the blood."

"She's being accused of his murder. That's par for this town." He paused. "I'll see her first thing in the morning and find out if I can divulge what I know."

Luke stroked his chin with his right thumb and forefinger. "Please make sure no one hears you mention my name. The less Chief Hopkins knows, the better it'll be." He paused. "I've got to do some serious praying for direction. This town is so obsessed with gossip and prejudice." He threw up his hands. "I just thank God for your friendship. I was beginning to think I would never make a difference in this town, but your encouragement to be the light the Lord desires has helped."

The pastor clasped his hands. "My mother always used to say a friend in need is a friend indeed."

"My mother always said the same thing. You know both parents were faithful to the Lord." His face screwed up. "I guess that's why it's so hard about May. When she was young, she seemed to love the Lord." He paused. "I've no idea what changed her. She doesn't even want me mentioning the Lord in her presence. However, I've decided I'm going to say whatever I believe the Lord wants me to say." He chuckled. "Besides, she lives in my house."

"I've been praying for her." The pastor paused and took a sip of his tea. "The rest is in the Lord's hands. However, I think we need to pray right now." Pastor O'Reilly bowed his head. "Lord, we need your wisdom to help us to know what to do for Elizabeth. She's your child, and only you can help her during this very trying time. We look to you for direction. In Jesus name, we pray."

"Amen!" They both said in unison.

"Well, I guess I better get to the diner to help May. The dishwasher is away, and I promised to help with the dishes. Besides, she must have my supper waiting. I don't have much of an appetite at present, but I think it's best if I act normal. I'm sure town gossip and the news will let her know soon enough." Luke stood up and pushed in his chair.

Pastor O'Reilly stood up, went over to Luke, and patted him on the shoulder. "Trust the Lord, for he knows the beginning and the end. He already has this thing wrapped up. We just have to follow his lead, and all will be fine."

Luke shook his head. "Like my mother always said. God knows the beginning and the ending and has it all in hand. He knows what he's doing. It's just us who can become impatient during the in between time, but faith knows enough to wait on the Lord." Luke combed back his curls with his right hand. "My mother always taught the importance of waiting on the Lord. She said if we don't wait, we could find ourselves giving birth to Ishmael. We know the problems Israel has endured all these years because Abraham and Sarah leaned unto their own understanding and didn't wait for God's promise."

"Amen! I would've loved to have known your mother. She seems to have been like mine." He clasped his hands together. "Well, they're both part of the great cloud of witnesses urging us on. What a great reunion day is ahead for the believers in Christ."

"That's for sure." Luke paused. "I guess I'll get to the diner. If you find out anything to help Elizabeth, please let me know."

"Like I said, I'll talk to her tomorrow morning. I'm sure she'll give me permission to tell you what I know. After I see her, I'll leave a message on your answering machine. In case May listens to it, I'll just say I have some chamomile tea. That will be your cue to come and see me."

§

Luke was still struggling with going to the diner after he left Pastor O'Reilly. Tonight, of all nights, he didn't wish to see his sister. But he promised to help while the dishwasher was away, and he wouldn't go back on his word. If only May would get a vision of the town's problem, instead of welcoming the gossip. When he pulled up, he saw May looking out the window. He knew she was wondering why he was late.

He walked into the diner and smiled. "Sorry I'm late, but I had something to do."

May gestured with her right hand. "Have a seat. I've kept a plate of roast beef for you." She poured him a coffee and set his plate. "The dishes are caught up, but I need you to put away the supplies." Luke's shoulders drooped as he sat on the stool. She eyed him curiously. "You look done in." Before he could respond, she turned on the television. "Let's see if there's anything on the news."

May's eyes bulged when she heard the special report. "Elizabeth Johnson was arrested this evening for the murder of her husband, Barth Johnson. Chief Hopkins told reporters that Officer Drake arrived on the scene to find the suspect holding the murder weapon. Although there is no official statement, this newsman believes it's an open-and-shut case."

"You found her with the weapon?" May said as she ran to hug him. "I must have all the details." She clapped her hands and did a little two-step. "How wonderful for business." She laughed. "Not that business is slow, but this will certainly spice things up. This is just the greatest news I've had for some time." She clapped her hands again. "This is all so delightful." She did a little hop. "My brother will be the hero of the town. Everyone will want to know how my brother found the murder weapon in her hands. You must give me all the details."

Luke's face ebbed of color. "Gossip does captivate most in this town."

"It's no surprise to me Elizabeth Johnson is accused of murdering her husband," she said in a holier-than-thou tone. "We all knew she'd be reckless someday." She gestured with her right hand. "Besides, I've thought she was nothing but trouble, with her uppity-nose, since they bought the old Vandyke Manor. She makes everyone who goes to your church uncomfortable. Hedy told me she acts as though she's the Virgin Queen or something. She follows the Pastor's reading in the Bible. I mean how ridiculous."

Luke stared at his food feeling his muscles tense. "I read along with the scriptures texts also. So, what am I called?"

"Everyone knows you just do what you do to honor our parents. But I truly wish you would stop going around quoting Bible verses. It's just a bunch of fictitious stories. I hoped you'd have grown out of it by now. After all, our parents died in that flu epidemic almost ten years ago. You don't have to please them any longer."

"I'm not going over this again. All I know is our parents loved the Lord and so do I." He gave out a heavy sigh. "My concern is why people are so nasty to Mrs. Johnson." His face screwed up. "Come on May. You know in your heart of hearts she's never bothered anyone. She's always kept to herself." He pushed his dinner away and got up. "It's a crying shame what this town has put her through."

"I can't share your sentiments. I've never liked her." May shook her head and stared at his food. "You should eat a little. After all, I promised our parents I would make sure you had a good lunch and a good dinner. At least eat for their sake."

Luke stared her in the eyes. "Eat for their sake, but I'm not to follow their lead in serving the Lord?" He gazed at his plate. "I've lost my appetite." He stood up. "If you'll excuse me, I'll put away the supplies. When I'm finished, I'll leave out the back door. I wouldn't want to interfere with you and Hedy's nightly entertainment."

Hedy Brown came into the diner as Luke entered the storeroom. Luke was disgusted when he heard the obvious joy in May's voice conveying Elizabeth's arrest for murdering her husband. When she gloated about Luke finding the murder weapon in her hand, he almost felt sick.

Hedy snickered at the news. "Luke will be the town hero with this news." She shook her head. "Poor Barth. He's received the brunt of Elizabeth's malicious temper for the five years this town's known them. None of our men would have put up with such a woman spending money like it grows on trees."

"Sure thing," May said, pouring Hedy a coffee.

Hedy took a sip. "Wasn't Barth some kind of an executive in Capital City?"

"He owned the company." May shook her head. "Too bad he came home this weekend. It's a crying shame a man like him would marry such a woman. I've never understood what he saw in her." She poured herself a coffee and sat next to Hedy. "I mean, she's an attractive blue-eyed blond and all that, but her uppity nose is a bit much." She took a sip of her coffee. "Barth must've worked hard to keep her in such an expensive lifestyle."

Hedy laughed and almost choked on her coffee. "I'll say. That snooty dame dresses in the latest fashions and drives a new Ferrari. I've never seen her do anything except spend money."

"Her husband's hard-earned dollars," May snorted.

Luke finished the supplies and went out the back door. He'd heard enough gossip for one night. If he didn't feel strongly about the Lord wanting him to do something in the town, he would have transferred to another police department long before now.

Chapter 3

The Town Hero

The next morning, the gossipmongers had the case wrapped up, and Luke was the town hero. He was congratulated for his quick response in finding the murder weapon in Elizabeth's hand. However, Luke wished he hadn't been the one to see anything. After all, he had admired the way she stayed above the chatter of the town. He couldn't believe she was capable of such a crime, and was determined to find the truth and prove her innocence.

Squeezing through his scandalmongering fans, Luke entered Chief Hopkins' office. "Chief," Luke said, trying to sound composed, "I'd like some of my vacation time. I didn't realize I'd accumulated so much. It seems you have everything tied up here, so I figured now's a good time." He combed back his curls with his right hand. "Of course, if it's acceptable to you. If it's not a problem, I'd like to take six weeks starting today." He gestured with his right hand.

"No problem, Drake," he said, puffing his cigar. "Detective division has found some facts that make the Johnson case airtight. It seems Barth Johnson was a drunk and gambler. She's a filthy rich heiress from New England, Boston area." He sat back in his chair.

"According to the butler, Barth wanted a larger allowance than she gave him. She was obviously fed up with his asking for money and lost her temper." The chief rocked his chair and snickered. "Well, her money won't buy her innocence. I've never cared for the way she made people feel uncomfortable. She was always so distant." He paused. "Trudy tried to get her involved in some of the town goings on, but she told her gossip displeased the Lord." He gestured at Luke. "My wife's probably as wealthy as her, but doesn't try to be holier-than-thou." He nodded with his head. "She seems to be your type." He laughed until his belly shook. "You can quote Bible verses together."

§

Luke couldn't wait to get home and check the answering machine. He listened to his messages and was relieved to hear Pastor O'Reilly had chamomile tea. He was grateful Mrs. Jeffers didn't clean their house on Monday. She had asked to clean Wednesday, Friday, and Saturday. If she had seen him getting his suitcases, she would have headed straight for the diner to tell May. He figured before he headed out to see the pastor, he would pack his suitcases. He had this strong impression the Lord wanted him to go to Capital City.

After loading the back of his Saturn Vue, he drove to the parsonage. Before he got out of his SUV, the pastor was standing on the front porch. "Luke am I glad to see you. How did you get time out of work? I know how Chief Hopkins is with you." He paused. "I think we better get inside." He rubbed the back of his neck with his right hand. "I remember the beaver in Narnia saying the trees were listening. In this town, there can be ears all over the place."

They both entered the parsonage, and the pastor locked his door. "Let's sit at the kitchen table" He led the way and gestured with right hand. "Have a seat. I've got my notes written down. I just finished writing them, when I felt the impression to look outside. I no sooner stepped onto the porch, and there you were pulling up." He clasped his hands together. "God is just so awesome." He paused. "Do you want some iced tea?"

"No, thank you. I guess I'm feeling a little anxious about this whole thing." He sat down on a chair. "The chief said the detectives discovered Barth was a drunk and a gambler. He said Elizabeth's a rich heiress from New England. Apparently, Barth received an allowance from her." He combed his hair back with his right hand. "They believe he wanted more money, she lost her temper, and killed him." He blew out a heavy sigh. "It's all quite bizarre. Why would she marry a drunk and a gambler?" His face screwed up. "I mean, I see her in church all the time. She seems to genuinely love the Lord."

"Well, I guess you know about everything. However, I can fill in the blanks the chief didn't." He paused. "I think I need a glass of iced tea. Are you sure you don't want one?"

Luke grinned. "Maybe I will. I am rather thirsty."

Pastor O'Reilly got them both a glass of iced tea and set one in front of Luke and one at his side. He sat down and picked up his notes. "Okay, Elizabeth met him while she was in college. He was a sharp dresser and knew how to carry himself. She was convinced he was a successful businessman. It's difficult for her to talk about it." He took a sip of his tea. "She comprehends she didn't seek the Lord about him. Apparently, she'd just lost her grandmother and was in grief." He paused. "Anyway, she knows there's no excuse for not seeking the Lord and realizes she was a young and foolish girl who let him sweep her off her feet." He rubbed the back of his neck with his right hand. "All her friends thought he was a looker which helped feed her foolishness."

"I understand we can all be deceived. But his drinking and gambling should have been a red flag the guy was no good."

"He pretended to be a non-drinker when around her." He took a drink of his iced tea. "She said he claimed people work too hard for their money to gamble it away."

Luke stroked his chin with his right thumb and forefinger. "The guy was a real snake." He paused. "However, you did say she didn't seek the Lord. If she had sought him whole-heartedly, he would have put a check in her spirit." He gestured towards the pastor. "You just preached that last week. The only way we can be deceived is because we choose to be. We allow what we want to get in the way of what the Lord wants. When we do that, we'll hear the counsel of our own heart and not the counsel of the Holy Spirit." He paused. "I'm not condemning Elizabeth. God knows how many times I've messed up. I'm the last one to judge her. I just wonder how many times we Christians find ourselves in a pickle because we didn't seek God?"

Pastor O'Reilly nodded his head. "Sometimes, Luke, I think you're in the wrong profession. However, when I prayed, the Lord made clear you're right where he wants you to be. I'll not question his wisdom." He paused. "Anyway, her whole life with Barth was a sham. It was all to cover up her embarrassment and sin of marrying a non-Christian."

"I don't understand why she stayed married to the leach. After all, it was her money and not his. Why did she continue the entire charade?"

"Elizabeth truly repented for not seeking God about marrying Barth, but believed she had to stay married as long as he did. The Bible says if the unbeliever is content to stay with the believer then the believer must continue in the marriage. He never beat her or did her any physical harm. She figured her unhappy marriage was the result of her sin. It seems they've not really been husband and wife since their honeymoon. Elizabeth just lived as though she was a virgin; she believed in being faithful to her marriage vows."

Luke stroked his chin with his right thumb and forefinger. "This is so sad. It's apparent she loves the Lord, and I believe he will make this all work out for her good. However, it doesn't look good now." He gestured with his right hand. "But we know faith doesn't look at what it sees, but what it doesn't see." He drank down his glass of tea. "I'm going to Capital City and see what I can found out. All night the Lord impressed upon me to go there. It was like when the Lord must needs go to Samaria." He chuckled. "Oh yes, you asked me how I managed to get time off work. I took some vacation. I didn't realize I had so much built up." He sat back and folded his arms. "The chief was quite eager for me to leave. I believe he'd like me out of his way with this investigation." He paused. "All

I can say is thank God he had me do it, because he knew I would need it now." He stood up and pushed his chair in place.

The pastor clasped his hands. "God is so awesome. I almost wish I could accompany you, but I must take care of my flock." He stood up and pushed in his chair. "If I find out anything of help, how can I get in touch with you?"

Luke reached into his pocket and pulled out a cell phone. "Last month, the Lord impressed me to get this. It must have been for this trip." He took out his notebook and pencil. "I'll write down the number for you." He wrote the number down and handed the paper to the pastor. "I don't have to worry about you giving it to anyone. I didn't let May know about it."

Pastor O'Reilly put his right hand on Luke's left shoulder. "Let's pray for you to have a fruitful trip." They both bowed their heads. "Lord Jesus, the only one who can lead Luke to find what is hiding in darkness is you. Please give him wisdom to follow your lead in all things. He's a man after truth, and only you can lead him to find it. We bind the powers of Hell trying to make it look as if Elizabeth is the murderer. Our spirits sense she's innocent, and we need you to give the light necessary to reveal what darkness is presently hiding. In Jesus name, we ask it. Amen."

"Amen!" Luke echoed. "Thank you, pastor. You have my number, and if I find something I need to run by you, I'll call you."

"Godspeed to you, Luke."

§

Luke sat in his car outside the diner contemplating what he heard from the chief. It was clear he had to do something to shatter the so-called airtight case against Elizabeth, but what to do was the question now. However, he knew the Lord was leading him to Capital City, so he would trust that leading. His struggle was with the detective division. Outside of Peter Pruitt and a couple of guys, he knew it wasn't all it was hyped-up to be, and there was no way he would have confidence in its findings. During his time on the force, the Lord had showed him many things the detectives had missed. But of course, the chief always took the credit.

He blew out a heavy sigh. "Well, I'd better stop procrastinating and get in the diner and tell May I'll be on vacation for a while. "Lord, I know it's probably wrong of me, but there are times I wish May had moved out of the house after our parents died." His face screwed up. "After all, the house was willed to me and the diner was willed to her." He shook his head. "I know Lord, how can I kick my sister out? Besides, I promised my dad as long as I was single, she could stay." He chuckled. "Even if she didn't live with me, her spies would know I left town." He combed back his black curls with his right hand. "Lord, please help me to tell her without actually telling her what I'm going to do." He got out of the car. "Better get it over with," he whispered as he entered the diner and saw no customers.

May's eyebrows scrunched together. "What are you doing here at this time?" She gestured towards the clock. "It's early, you don't eat until one. Are you taking an early lunch? Do you want something to eat?" She poured him a coffee. "Do you want today's special?"

"No," he said wanting to get to the point. "I just wanted to stop by and talk for a few minutes." He sat down. "Have you ever felt things aren't as they seem?"

"What do you mean? Are you talking in general or in particular?" She gave a glare of perception. "Wait a minute! Do you mean the Johnson case?" She gave him a scowl. "She's as guilty as blood." She gestured with her right hand. "Come off it, Luke." She gave out a heavy sigh. "For crying out loud, you're the one who found the murder weapon in her hands." She placed her hands on her hips. "The old saying, seeing is believing says it all. You know that. You're a police officer and you deal in facts. Since when did details become irrelevant?"

"She claims to be innocent. I heard her tell the chief she found him on the floor with the bust next to him. She didn't realize anything was amiss until she picked it up and saw blood."

"What a crock of crap. She's as innocent as the devil himself. You're letting little Miss Pretty blur your vision. Wake up to truth before you become the laughingstock of the town."

Taking his keys out of his pocket, Luke swallowed a lump in his throat. "I'll be out of town for a few weeks. Haven't used any vacation time in a long while, I felt I needed to get away for a bit. I've asked the chief for the time, and he said there was no problem." Drinking down his coffee, he put the cup down before continuing. "It seems he thinks the Johnson case is tied up. He said something about money or something. Anyway, I can't put my finger on what is bothering me about this whole thing. So, I thought perhaps I've been working too much and need some time off." He gave her a kiss on the cheek.

"Yes, I think you've been working too much. You take a vacation and get your thoughts together. Once you rest, you'll see things more clearly."

Chapter 4

The Clues Mount Up

L uke prayed all the way to Capital City. "Lord, help me see what you want me to see. I have to keep my wits about me, not miss any clue, and know what to do with what I find." He looked at his directions. "The building should be on the left side of this street. Yes, there it is." He paused. "I should have expected it to be quite an impressive building. How could I assume anything less with them owning the most prestigious manor around?" He sighed as he got out of his vehicle and headed for the main entrance to the building." Luke was somewhat baffled that it appeared empty. As he perused the inside of the building, he noticed a slim man about sixty cleaning. He went over to him and showed his identification. "I'm Luke Drake from the Burroughville Police. I'm here about Barth Johnson's murder."

"I'm Martin Phillips, the janitor." He paused. "I was surprised ta hear about the murder." He scratched the back of head with his left hand. "If ya follow me, I'll show his apartment."

"Yes, please. I guess that's a good place to start."

Martin showed Luke up to Barth's apartment located on the third floor, unlocked the door, and let him in.

Luke combed back his curls with his right hand as he spied out the apartment. He saw a bedroom, a living room, and a kitchen. In the living room, he spotted a plush sofa, a recliner, a sixty inch television with surround sound, a desk, a phone, an answering machine, and a couple of cases of scotch. The kitchen had a table and chairs, a coffee maker, a refrigerator, a stove, a microwave oven, and a toaster oven. Luke smelled a rat. This big capital executive had a home away from home. Why would he want to live away from a wife like Elizabeth? But the Pastor did say they weren't really husband and wife in the real sense.

Martin watched as Luke took in the room. "Ya cops trying ta pin the murder on Elizabeth? Don't think she dun it." He scratched the back of his head with his left hand. "After the wife died, I was dun with brick laying. Elizabeth didn't care I had no experience. Said I could be trusted. It was her which told him ta hire me. Got the feeling he didn't like it." He shook his head. "Never could figure how a sweet lady got mixed up with such a loser." He pointed to the mess all around with a couple of cases of scotch against the wall and empty bottles strewn all over. "He was never in his office. Was always here with his girlfriend. If I didn't know better, I woulda thought she was his wife."

"Did you say girlfriend?" Luke was suddenly attentive. "What do you mean?"

"A decked out doll. Kept her looking like a million bucks. She was always by his side." He scratched the back of his head with his left hand. "Never cared for her. Always rude. Acted as if she was the boss." He gestured with both hands. "Have no idea what kinda company it is. Outside of his delivery of scotch, Mrs. Johnson coming in once a month ta pay the bills and givin me my salary, I don't see nobody." He paused. "Oh yea, he's got a short stocky friend who comes sometimes."

Luke combed back his black curls with his right hand. "Really!" He paused. "Do you know the girlfriend's name? Where can I find her?"

"Nope. Haven't seen her since his death." He headed for the door. "Don't know the friend's name neither." He gestured with his left hand. "I'll let ya investigate." He paused. "Must admit I was surprised nobody's been here ta ask questions. Seemed awful slack for police not ta come." He shook his head as he opened the door. "Had ta speak my mind."

Luke gave a blithe gesture with his right hand. "It's fine. I understand."

Alone in the apartment, Luke was aghast at the eyesore. "Lord, Martin said no detectives have been here. Is that why you wanted me to come? Please help me to see what I'm supposed to see in all this mess." He stroked his chin with his right thumb and forefinger. "I know Elizabeth married him without praying for direction. But why would she make everyone think he had the money? Why did she hide he was a drunk and gambler?" He paused. "I know Pastor O'Reilly said she felt her unhappy marriage was the result of her marrying a non-Christian." He blew out a heavy sigh. "Why make everyone think she was spending her husband's money?" He glared around once again. "Wait a minute! Martin said he had a girlfriend living here with him. How come nothing was mentioned about Barth having a girlfriend? Lord, is this why I'm here? Where do I begin? Please give me direction."

Just then his eyes caught sight of the answering machine next to the phone. He hurried over to it, checked for messages, turned it on, and heard. "Barth, this is Wayne. See you Monday night outside the Casino Quattro at eight. Don't be late. I think you'll enjoy this game."

Luke looked at his watch. "It's now seven o'clock." He quickly checked the phone book for the casino's address and then checked his city map for its location.

§

He tried to stay calm as he drove there. "Lord, please let Wayne be there. I don't know who he is, but he's obviously a friend of Barth's. Perhaps he's the friend Martin mentioned. If so, he must know the name of the girlfriend." His tires squealed slightly as he pulled up to the casino. The cop in him kept his emotions calm as the valet took his car. Spotting two men standing near the front door, he walked over to them, and flashed his identification. "I'm Luke Drake of the Burroughville Police. Do either of you know Wayne? I have some questions to ask him about Barth Johnson?"

The short stocky one smiled. "I'm Wayne Olson. You're the officer who found the murder weapon in Elizabeth's hand. I don't forget names. I figured someone would look to talk to me. Well, it looks like you didn't waste too much time in finding me. I wasn't sure if I had to go to the Burroughville Police Station myself."

"What do you mean?"

"Barth was a rogue. I felt I owed him my life, but I'm not obligated to keep quiet any more. I wish I'd listened to my wife and told Elizabeth before she married him, but I didn't. I guess it's something I'll regret the rest of my life." He folded his arms. "I just called Barth a rogue, but I was probably worse for not telling Elizabeth." Wayne exhaled heavily. "You see, while we were in the army, Barth saved my life." He looked around. "Could we go someplace to talk? I really need to get this off my chest."

"You'll have to lead the way. I don't know this part of the city." He paused. "I've been on the southside many times, but I've never been in this part before."

Wayne pointed across the street. "That coffee shop's usually empty at this hour."

They both ordered a coffee and sat in a corner booth. Wayne spoke first. "Elizabeth took a lot of abuse from Barth. I was with him at the Malaney Restaurant when they met. He liked to play the role even after he'd gambled away his settlement. It's a long story, but I'll give the abridged version. His parents were killed by a drunk driver. The guy was wealthy, Barth sued and won millions."

He sipped his coffee as if pondering where to go next. "Elizabeth was about to graduate from college. She and a few classmates were treating some professors to a fancy lunch. Barth had an eye for money. Of course, Elizabeth's nice looking, but her wealth was his attraction. When it came to women, he preferred tall, dark-eyed, brunettes. I sat there while he lied about being a successful businessman. Old Barth had a way of sweet-talking a baby out of his bottle." He paused. "What really haunts me is that Elizabeth is the sweetest thing; she wouldn't hurt anyone." He bit the hangnail on his right thumb. "You see, she's a Christian and reminds me so much of my mother. How could I let Barth do that to her? I feel as if I allowed it to happen to my mother. If my mother was alive, she wouldn't be too happy with me." He touched Luke's right hand. "You see, I know better. Instead of thinking I owed Barth something for saving my life, it's the Lord who deserves the thanks. How did I allow myself to get tangled up with such a wicked person and be corrupted by his evil communications? My mother would have said I moved my tent too close to Sodom." He sat back; his gaze etched with sadness.

Luke tapped the table with his fingers, he wasn't sure if any of this would help Elizabeth. He already knew she was the one with the money. "This doesn't tell me anything." Luke's tone revealed his frustration. "Detective division knows she's the one with the money, and he was a drunk and gambler. I don't mean to sound irritated, but is this going to prove her innocent?"

Wayne's eyebrows scrunched together. "Officer Drake, you seem to be taking a personal interest in things. You're a little too uptight for someone who's supposed to be investigating this crime."

"Wait a minute," Luke chuckled. "I'm supposed to get the information." He folded his arms, sat back, and stared at Wayne. "To be truthful, I can't believe she's guilty. Yet, it seems the more I hear, I'm not sure what to think. I know the most peaceful person can hit a boiling point if they're not careful. Believe me, I don't know how much of a guy like him anyone could take." He paused. "Is there anything else you can tell me?"

"She's an incredible lady to have put up with what she did. When Barth told me she was devastated on their honeymoon, he laughed. By the time they married, he had borrowed up to his neck. If she hadn't bailed him out, he'd have been in big trouble with some loan sharks." He paused, wiped the sweat from his brow and took a deep breath. "But that's not what I'm trying to get at. There's something troubling me."

"Let's hope it disturbs me too."

"It seems his girlfriend has moved out or left town."

"How do you know?"

"Did you find any of her things in Barth's apartment? I have a key."

"What's so important about the girlfriend's belongings?"

"After I heard he was dead, I felt strongly to check out the apartment. It was about midnight, but I knew Madeline didn't stay there when he was gone. I have no idea where she went. But when I looked around, I noticed all her little trinkets were missing. Anyway, I checked the bedroom, and her clothes were gone. Any sign of a female sharing the place was wiped clean. Why would she move out? She was bonkers over Barth and would never leave him. She's been after him to divorce Elizabeth for years. Of course, he wasn't about to give up his bank account. He claimed Elizabeth was a money hungry witch, and if he tried to leave, she'd sue him for his pants."

"What are you getting at?" Luke said, throwing up his hands in anguish.

Wayne leaned forward. "Office Drake where's your detective skills? Why would she move her stuff out the day he's murdered? Barth had called me Friday afternoon to remind me he'd be gone this weekend. I heard him ask her to get his suitcase ready."

Luke's heart was palpitating in his chest. Was there any possible link to this? "Do you know anything else about her? Where she worked? Who her friends are?"

"I don't know a thing about her other than she was his painted doll. Every time I saw her, she was always with Barth. I never saw her alone."

"What about his secretary? Would she know?"

"Secretary? He didn't have a secretary. What would he need a secretary for?"

Luke stroked his chin with his right thumb and forefinger. "Could you give me a description of the girlfriend? What's her name?"

After a few more questions, Luke was sure of Elizabeth's innocence. "Thank you, Wayne. I believe you've been an incredible help. If I have any more questions, where can I reach you?"

Wayne gave him his telephone number. "If my wife, Jane, answers, you can tell her whatever. She knows about everything. It was her who helped me see it wasn't Barth I owed my life to, but the Lord." He paused. "You see, Barth had promised to set me up when he hit it big. In my deception, I hung on." He bit the hangnail on his right thumb. "But I knew he couldn't hold on to money; it slipped through his hands like water." He wiped the sweat off his forehead. "My mother always said obsolete dreams need to wash out to sea like sandcastles." He clenched his jaw. "What a fool I was to hang onto what I knew would never transpire. Why do we deceive ourselves?"

Luke shook Wayne's hand. "It seems we both had godly mothers. Thank God for mothers who lead us on the straight and narrow."

"Amen! I should have followed her advice." Wayne said, as he motioned to the waiter and asked for the bill.

Chapter 5

Truth Reveals What Darkness Hides

Luke stayed at a motel for the night and headed back first thing in the morning. He had to do first things first and tie up some loose ends, before he made a move. If he left anything undone, the chief would take the credit. He'd do a license plate check for ownership, verify a name, get an address, and then clarify some points with Harold Simpson. However, first he wanted to let Pastor O'Reilly know what transpired. Maybe he could help him see something he may have missed.

When he pulled up to the parsonage, Pastor O'Reilly was just entering through the door. He turned around, saw Luke, and motioned with his right hand for him to come in. He led Luke into the kitchen and gestured for him to take a seat. "Luke, I didn't expect you back so quickly." He clasped his hands together. "You just left yesterday. I sure hope you have some good news. This town sounds like a lynching mob." He paused. "I'm overwhelmed at people calling themselves Christians and behaving like the devil. Some of them can't know the Lord. I believe some may be backsliding.

It's like Lot moving his tent too close to Sodom. When Christians allow themselves to listen to gossip day in and day out they soon become partakers of the tittle-tattle and start spreading it themselves." He rubbed the back of his neck with his right hand. "My mother always said it's this thing in people wanting to be liked by other people. But Christians should only be concerned about being liked by the Lord. If God is first, then they won't be overtaken by the crowd's vices and join them. Of course, it's based on scripture which says friendship with the world is enmity against God. Let me put it in simple terms. If we love the world more than we love God, we choose to be God's enemy." He gave out a heavy sigh. "I do believe I haven't given you a chance to get a word in edge wise. As you can see, I've been dumbfounded at the negativity pointed at Elizabeth, when I'm convinced in my heart she's innocent."

"I believe once I clarify a few things, we'll have the proof. I'm sure the light of truth reveals what darkness hides. It seems Barth had a girlfriend who lived with him in Capital City named Madeline Owens. From what Barth's army buddy, Wayne Olson, told me, she was after Barth to divorce Elizabeth. Apparently, she was getting fed up with the situation. Wayne told me the day Barth was murdered, she moved out of his apartment. Why would she move out? There's not a trace in the apartment of her ever living there." He paused. "Wayne's having a tough time of it. He knew Barth was a drunk and gambler, but he just remained silent and watched his shenanigans. He told me Elizabeth found out what he was on their honeymoon and had to bail him out." He gestured with his hands. "It seems some loan shark was going to take him out. When Barth told Wayne about the episode and Elizabeth's devastation, he laughed. Now, he's having a hard time. He wishes he'd told Elizabeth about Barth before she married him, but he thought he owed Barth."

"Why would he owe Barth?"

"They were in the Army together and Barth saved his life. Now, Wayne knows he owes the thanks for his life to the Lord and not Barth." He combed back his black curls with his right hand. "However, from what Wayne said, I believe Barth must have pushed the belief on him. Wayne told me Barth was a smooth talker who could con a baby out of his bottle." He shook his head. "Apparently, Barth told him he'd set him up when he hit it big. He's having a difficult time at allowing himself to be so deceived."

"I try not to say ill of anyone, but he was a scoundrel. Elizabeth told me about the honeymoon, and they haven't been husband and wife since then. He told her he didn't love her. He laughed, said he loved her money, and he expected her to keep her marriage vows to him. He said a good Christian woman like her wouldn't lie in the presence of God." He paused. "What she's been through. Yet, she's convinced God is working on her behalf to prove her innocence and believes truth will reveal what's hiding in the darkness." He gestured towards Luke with his right hand. "I told her about you and your going to Capital City to see what you could find out. She was grateful for a true man of God in this town. I told her there are more, but they've been conned into moving their tent too close to Sodom and its evil. Once their eyes are opened, they'll see truth. I've been praying for the Holy Spirit to get a hold of the people who deep down in their heart want to please God. I'm convinced he'll do it. I talk to a lot of people, and I feel in my spirit some are not content grieving the Holy Spirit. God is going to do something wonderful in this town."

"As you were speaking, I felt the Holy Spirit declare to my spirit, 'stand still and see the salvation of the Lord.' I have this overwhelming sense of expectation in me."

The pastor clasped his hands. "Yes!" He touched Luke's right shoulder. "Luke, my boy, I believe God is going to bust this town wide open with revival. Something good is in store. We just have to remain steadfast in our prayers for it to happen."

"Well, I have to get to the manor and talk to Elizabeth's butler. I have a few things to clarify before I can proceed." He put out his right hand. "Pray I have a prosperous journey."

Pastor O'Reilly shook Luke's hand. "His Holy Spirit will guide your steps. Remember, God's light dispels all darkness. Whatever may be hidden will be revealed."

"Amen!" Luke nodded. "Thank you for your words of encouragement." He gestured with his hands. "The Bible says with God nothing shall be impossible. What a comfort his word can be." He paused. "It's encouraging to know what can seem overwhelming to us is like nothing to God."

"Amen!"

§

Luke was singing *Onward Christian Soldiers* as he drove to the manor to speak to the butler. When he pulled up to the entrance, he was reminded of his last visit. He could still see the smirk on the chief's face and his pleasure at arresting Elizabeth. "Lord, I don't want to seem judgmental, but I pray you take the smirk off the chief's face. I think we've been allowing the ungodly to push us down for too long. Help us to stand in your full armor against the evil in this town and do it with your grace. Let hearts be pricked with your love, enable them to see the error of their way, and repent. Hell was not created for people, but for the devil and his demons. Open the eyes of the spiritually blind to see that living in defiance to your word as the devil did, will find them spending eternity in Hell."

Luke got out of his SUV and walked up the front door. Before he rang the doorbell, the door opened. "Officer Drake," Harold said. "I realized who you were when you stepped out of your 4x4." He gestured with his right hand. "Please come in." He led Luke to the Kitchen where this petite woman with silver hair was standing near the counter. Harold gestured towards the woman. "This is my wife, Sarah."

Sarah reached out with her right hand. "Nice to meet you. I've seen you in church and heard so much about you." Her face beamed. "It's all been good. First, Harold told me about the night of the arrest, Pastor O'Reilly told me about you when I brought some items to the church, and then Harold was told about you by Miss Elizabeth."

Harold scratched the back of his head with his right hand. "We'll be glad to answer any questions you may have. You see, Miss Elizabeth told me about you when I visited her in the pokey." He grinned. "It seems she was telling me about you while Pastor O'Reilly was telling Sarah about you. Anyway, I wasn't sure if they would let me see her, so I told them, I needed some information." He gestured with his right hand. "Anyway, she whispered what Pastor O'Reilly told her about you, and that you were heading to Capital City to see what you could find out." He paused. "Then, I whispered that I could tell you were having a bona fide tough time the night of her arrest. The condescending remarks of the chief about your faith made me know you were an honest police officer." He motioned for Luke to have a seat. "Please sit down. Sarah and I were just about to have a spot of tea. Miss Elizabeth buys us loose-leaf teas from China. They're really quite nice." He gave out a heavy sigh. "She would be having a cup with us if she was home. I believe she looks at us as adopted parents. Her parents died when she was very young. After their death, her grandmother raised her and took care of her fortune until she was twenty-one. Eight months after her twenty-first birthday, her grandmother passed away." He paused. "She was grieving her grandmother when the serpent came into her life." He threw up his right hand. "I think I have to get off the subject of that blaggard and have my tea." He pointed to a chair. "Please sit down and have a spot of tea with us."

Luke couldn't help but notice the contrast between the man and his wife. Harold stood about six feet in stature weighing close to two-hundred pounds; whereas, Sarah, weighing about a hundred pounds, didn't make five feet. Luke turned towards Sarah. "What can you tell me?"

Gazing at him through pale blue eyes, she sighed. "I'm glad he's gone. Didn't wish the blaggard harm, but he was a wicked man. I never liked him. We stayed on to be of help to Miss Elizabeth." Tears filled her eyes. "Poor soul needed someone to comfort her. She had no family, so we sort of adopted her."

Luke listened to Sarah and prayed he would find the truth and brighten up Elizabeth's life.

"Excuse me," Harold said, "but can we get on with our tea?"

"Thank you; I do enjoy tea more than coffee." Luke sat down. "I have some questions to ask of you about that night." He took out his notepad. "What I didn't understand is where the other servants were when I arrived? I know there are more. Not much gets past this town." His face screwed up. "How come there aren't any others here tonight?"

Harold addressed his wife. "Sarah would you pour our tea? I believe we can talk more comfortably with our tea."

"I quite agree a spot of tea will help calm us down. We need to stay unruffled and let the Lord lead us." She twisted her hands. "I'm quite uncomfortable with Miss Elizabeth being in the pokey. She wouldn't hurt anyone." She gestured with her hands. "If you could have seen how unpleasant he was to her, and she would just stand there with her head hung. But I'll give her credit for her strength in the Lord. She knew she was not to give him any more money, and she held firm. No yelling or anything. She would just fold her arms and shake her head."

Sarah poured their tea and Harold continued. "Now, let me tell you where the rest of the staff was that night." He sipped his tea. "You see, whenever Barth was going to be here, we gave them the weekend off. After all the trouble caused with their calling the police when Barth would start his trouble, it was easier for just me and Sarah to be here." He gestured towards Sarah. "Sarah and I were the only two she confided in. It seems the others were in on the town gossip and believed Miss Elizabeth was the culprit. It was the blind leading the blind. When you're deceived, you cannot see what is really happening in front of your eyes. Barth was swearing and demanding more money. When she refused to give him anymore, he became argumentative. He was a devil of a man. The servants saw the opposite through their deceived eyes." He paused. "I keep wishing Sarah and I were here Sunday night. But we were invited to a cookout for the butlers and their wives at the Mayor's house." He took a sip of his tea and sat back. "This tea is so refreshing." He took another sip. "As to why there aren't any other servants here now, Miss Elizabeth asked us to send them on a two month vacation to wherever they wanted to go. She said to spare no expense. They were told they would know if they still have a job when they get back. If not, they'll receive six months wages." He took another sip of his tea. "She doesn't believe she'll retain any of them. Can't say I blame her."

Luke's face screwed up. "Why is she called *Miss Elizabeth* and not Mrs. Johnson?"

Sarah hung her head. "She felt that name associated her with her sin and wanted to avoid it as much as possible."

Luke nodded and was busy taking down notes when he felt something rub his leg and meow. He tensed as a black cat jumped onto his lap.

"Well, I'll be." Harold laughed. "Aurora doesn't like men to well. She doesn't mind being in the same room with me, but that's it. That blaggard did something to her as a kitten which ended her going near men." He scratched the back of head with his right hand. "This is rather amazing. She's actually sitting on your lap."

Sarah joined in. "Well, Officer Drake, she must sense another spirit in you like she does in my Harold. That does beat all."

Harold got up from his chair and went to the kitchen cabinet. When he returned, he handed Luke a container of cat food. "Please see if you can get her to eat. We've been worried about her since Miss Elizabeth was arrested. She hasn't touched anything. They're quite attached to each other. I believe it would be too much for Miss Elizabeth to lose Aurora after all that's gone on."

"This cat," Luke chuckled, "I believe is more devoted than we'll ever understand. If I'm not mistaken, I believe she pointed out the murderer to me the night of the crime."

Sarah grabbed her heart with both hands. "Does that mean you know who murdered Barth?"

"Not yet, but I believe I know how to find out." He put Aurora on the floor. "Right now, I have a cat to feed." He put the food in front of the cat, and she began to eat.

"Well, I'll be," Harold laughed. Thank God you came here. She hasn't eaten anything since Sunday morning. Wait until I tell Miss Elizabeth about this." He paused. "I had to tell her we couldn't get her to eat. It's been a couple of days. She didn't even drink a little milk which she never refuses. This will brighten Miss Elizabeth up."

Luke, Harold, and Sarah were all quite gleeful as they enjoyed their tea and watched Aurora eat all her food. As soon as the cat finished, she jumped back up onto Luke's lap. "I think this cat wants to thank me for taking Elizabeth's innocence seriously." He picked her up and looked in her eyes. "Well, Aurora, I have to get going. If I'm going to get this accomplished, I need to get busy." He put the cat down and addressed the Simpson's. "Thank you for being such a help. I believe I have enough to go on. Please pray for the truth to reveal what has been hidden in the darkness."

Sarah grabbed her heart with both hands. "Officer Drake, that's what we've been praying. Pastor O'Reilly told me about the situation and how we needed the Lord to bring to light what has been hiding in the darkness." She paused. "I believe God has already started; for what seems impossible to man is possible to God."

"Amen!" Harold said. You see, Officer Luke, my wife's a woman of God." He grinned. If she wasn't, God wouldn't have told me to marry her."

Luke followed them to the front door, and they followed him to his car. When Luke opened his door, a flash of black jumped in before him and sat on the passenger seat. "I guess Aurora wants to come with me."

Sarah put up her right hand. "Let me get her food. Miss Elizabeth won't want you buying food for her cat. Besides, Aurora is rather fussy; she likes what she likes and that's it." Sarah hurried into the house and brought out a box. "I've got her food, her water bowl, her toys, her litter box with litter, and her little bed. She likes to sleep in it during the day. Of course, at night, she sleeps with Miss Elizabeth"

Luke laughed. "Do you mean she'll want to sleep in bed with me?"

Harold grinned. "Probably will. She likes to sleep at the top of the bed between the pillows. She's done that since she was a kitten."

Luke put the box in the back and got into the driver's seat. "I'll get back to you if I need any more information. Let Elizabeth know I'll take good care of Aurora until she gets home."

§

On the way home, Luke looked at the cat. "I'm not sure what I'm doing with you. My sister will probably have a fit. It's a good thing the house is mine and not hers. I know you usually stay clear of men, but I would suggest you stay clear of May." When he got home, he took Aurora upstairs to his bedroom and then retrieved her belongings. When he opened his bedroom door, he found Aurora curled up between the pillows. "What are you doing there now, it's still early?" He paused. "I understand. It's been quite an ordeal. You probably need some rest." He chuckled. "You're finally able to be at ease and have a full belly. A full belly is enough to make anyone need a siesta." He put her bed down with her toys and looked around. "I think I'll put this litter box and your water bowl in my bathroom, and put your food in my linen closet." He gestured towards the door. "I'll leave the door closed for now. I don't want May to find you if I'm not home." He blew out a heavy sigh. "I really need to do some investigating on this without alarming anyone about what I'm doing."

Luke sat at the bottom of his bed. "Lord, how can I get this information without the wrong people knowing?" He grabbed his head with both hands. "That's it. Thank you, Lord. Mitchell Cooke in the computer room is a godly man and we've had some good conversations. I'll go to his house tonight and see what can be done." He rubbed his stomach with his right hand. "Boy, I'm feeling quite hungry, but I don't want to face May at present. The chicken place on the outskirts of town is pretty good. Besides, it's closer to Mitchell's house." He gazed at Aurora. "I'm going to get something to eat before I see Mitchell. I'll see you later tonight when I get back. For now, you rest until we can get Elizabeth out of jail."

Chapter 6

Light Shines On the Darkness

Luke was quite relieved when he entered Tommy's Chicken Hut and didn't recognize anyone. Although it was only about five miles from the center of town, he didn't know anybody. He knew it was God, for he'd been on the force for almost ten years. He sat at a table, picked up the menu, and the waitress came over to him. "Can I get your order?"

Luke quickly eyed the menu. "I think number 5 will do just fine."

"Will you have anything to drink?"

"Yes, I would like some iced tea."

The waitress brought him his iced tea. When his meal was ready, she brought it to him. He ate his food and was pleased to eat without anyone asking him any questions. It was difficult, at times, to eat in peace at May's. Luke took out his notepad and looked at his notes; he wanted to be prepared when he talked to Mitchell.

§

When Luke arrived at Mitchell's house, he was quite impressed. It was a lovely ranch-style house with a wide covered deck. To the right of the back of the house was a large oak tree with a double swing. Set way back on the left was a fenced in chicken coop with chickens wandering around and pecking at bugs in the dirt. The front yard was well-manicured with a white picket fence.

Luke just sat back in his vehicle relaxing in the peace of the scene. "Lord, thank you for this serene feeling. I've been a little uptight of late with the gossip and prejudice of the town." He blew out a heavy sigh. "Of course, this thing about Elizabeth has my mind working overtime to prove her innocence. Help me to rest in you; for only you know what must be done. Lead me by your Holy Spirit and not my feelings of respect for Elizabeth." Luke was startled by Mitchell walking towards him. He opened his door and stepped out. "I hope I'm not interfering with you and your wife, but I really needed to talk to you."

Mitchell's eyebrows scrunched together. "It's no problem. I'm more interested in what would bring you out here." He grinned. "I've lost count of how many times I've invited you to stop by." He gestured towards the house. "Please come in. Margie is just finishing supper; you're more than welcome to join us. You can tell me what you have to talk about over some good home cooking." He rubbed his hands together. "Margie has won some country cooking contests. No brag, but she's the best cook in these parts." He put up his hands. "No offense to May. She can cook, but Margie's a professional."

"I'm not really hungry, but I'll join you. Just don't get upset if I don't eat much." He combed back his curls with his right hand. "I just ate at Tommy's Chicken Hut before coming here."

"Well, I better tell Margie. If I don't, she'll be piling up your plate."

Luke followed Mitchell into the house. Once inside, he sensed the same peace he felt outside. He knew Mitchell and Margie went to Burroughville Christian Fellowship Church like he did, but it must be because they serve the Lord. The turmoil he often felt at home had to be May's indifference to the Lord.

Margie came over to Luke with her right hand out. "It's so good to see you, Luke." She paused. "Am I supposed to call you Officer Drake?"

"Luke is just fine. I'm not on any official business." He stroked his chin with his right thumb and forefinger. "I do have some official business to discuss, but it has to remain between us. That's why I came out here. I didn't want to give place for anyone to hear it at the precinct."

Margie gestured with her right hand. "Please, let's go eat. We can talk after our meal. I don't want anything to get cold." She pointed to a chair on the right side of the table. "Luke, you can sit there." She then proceeded towards the stove to take something out of the oven. "I hope you like lasagna." She placed it on the table and went to the refrigerator. "I made a spinach salad to go with it." Margie then proceeded towards the top oven. "Of course, we can't have lasagna without garlic bread."

Mitchell laughed. "I think you should know Luke ate at the Chicken Hut before coming here. He may not be very hungry."

Margie put her hands on her hips. "Well, Luke, that was unsociable of you."

Luke's face flushed. "I'm sorry. I wasn't thinking of eating here. I hadn't eaten since yesterday, I felt quite hungry, and stopped there to eat. I wasn't up to seeing May just yet."

Margie's stomach shook with laughter. "I was only joshing with you. It's fine. Just eat what you can."

Luke blew out a heavy sigh. "You had me going there for a minute." He let out a laugh until his stomach shook. "I do believe I needed that. Whew! I can't remember the last time I really had a good laugh. Things have been quite stressful of late."

Mitchell rubbed his hands together. "Let's eat. I'm quite interested as to why you came here."

Margie sat down and quickly stood up. "I forget the iced tea." She paused. "Luke, if you prefer something else, let me know."

"Iced tea is fine."

She poured them all a glass of iced tea and sat back down. "Help yourself to the salad and lasagna." She smiled. "That way, I won't give you too much."

Luke took a bite of his lasagna. "Wow! What do you put in it to make it so delicious?" He gestured towards Mitchell with his right hand. "You said she was not just a cook, but a professional. I can't wait to taste the spinach salad and garlic bread."

"I told you no one can cook like my Margie. She's the best."

Luke gestured with both hands. "How can a spinach salad taste so special? You must have a supernatural touch from the Lord." He took a bite of the garlic bread. "Okay, this is incredible. I've had lasagna, spinach salad, and garlic bread many times at the diner, but never have I tasted anything like this." He gave a slow grin. "Do you mind if I take some more?"

Margie chuckled. "You may eat all you can."

When they finished eating, everyone cleaned up. Mitchell rubbed his hands together. "I think we should go into the parlor, and finally hear what you want to talk about."

Luke was amazed how simple colonial furniture could look so rich and at the same time be so cozy. He sat in a Queen Anne type colonial wing-chair, while Mitchell and Margie both sat on a woven damask, tapestry fabric, colonial sofa with lovely blue and white cushions. On the left side of the couch was a maple end table with a drawer in front. On the right side was a maple dovetailed dough box. In front of the sofa was a maple drop-leaf coffee table with a large drawer. Luke sighed. "Your house is so calm and cozy. It's the same peace I felt as I sat in my car before Mitchell came out."

Margie smiled. "That's because we ask the Lord's peace to touch all our visitors who welcome it."

Mitchell gave a wide grin. "Now, let's know what brought you out here."

Luke took out his notepad and flipped through the pages. "It's about the Johnson murder. I've been doing some investigating of my own." He paused. "I don't believe Elizabeth is guilty. That's why I need your help without anyone knowing what we're doing. You can look up a license plate number without others catching on. If I'm not mistaken, I believe the license plate number will reveal the murderer." He stroked his chin with his right thumb and forefinger. "You know if the chief catches on, he'll dismiss it. He's not going to accept anything coming from me. Besides, he's delighted to have made the arrest. He won't appreciate anyone proving him wrong."

Margie leaned forward. "Luke, we can't be concerned about what the chief thinks or doesn't think. It's more important to find the truth." She looked at her husband. "We don't believe she did it. We spoke to Pastor O'Reilly last night when we had him here for dinner and he told us about you going to Capital City. He asked us to pray you have a prosperous journey." Her eyebrows scrunched together. "However, we're amazed you're back already. God must have answered our prayer."

"I believe he did. He directed his light on the darkness."

Mitchell nodded. "I have no problem with looking up the number for you. We've been praying for the Lord to bring to light what has been hiding in darkness. If we pray for something, we better be willing to do whatever the Lord wants us to do."

Luke tore out a page from his notepad and wrote the license plate number. "This is the number of the plate of a red Toyota." He paused. "I better give you the number of my new cell phone. When you get the information, I don't want you calling my house. May will be wondering why you would be calling." He wrote down the phone number and handed the paper to Mitchell.

"I'll get on it first thing in the morning before anyone comes in. Everyone knows I get to work early to set up." He rubbed his hands together. "God is so good." He gave a wide grin. "I'll have the information before seven."

Luke stood up. "I better be going. Aurora is in a strange place, and I don't want her getting too nervous."

Mitchell eyebrows scrunched together. "I know it's none of my business, but did you say Aurora?"

Luke chuckled. "She's Elizabeth's cat, and the one responsible for my having the license plate number of the red Toyota. I've no idea how it was done, but God performed a miracle through that cat the night of the murder." He paused. I truly believe the owner of the car murdered Barth. Only God could have had her stop in front of my squad car." He combed back his curls with his right hand. "Anyway, it seems the cat hadn't eaten anything since before the arrest. When I visited Harold and Sarah Simpson, Aurora jumped on my lap. Harold said the cat was afraid of men after what Barth did to her as a kitten." He threw up his hands. "They were amazed when she let me feed her. As I was about to leave, she jumped in my car. I have her in my bedroom right now." He paused. "She likes me. Harold said it'll put Elizabeth's mind at rest with Aurora eating."

Margie put her hands on her hips. "That cat is proving you have a different spirit than Barth Johnson had."

"That's what Sarah Simpson said." He blew a heavy sigh. "I have the Lord to thank for the different spirit." He paused. "Well, I'll look to hear from you in the morning." Luke's face screwed up. "On second thought, I believe the Lord wants me to meet you here tomorrow. I sense God doesn't want us to give place to the devil."

Mitchell shook his head. "I quite agree. The Lord impressed me to have you come here, far away from any possible eavesdroppers."

"Good. What time do you want me here?"

Mitchell gazed at Margie.

Margie nodded. "If you don't mind eating my cooking two days in a row, you can be here for six."

"I think I can force myself to eat here again tomorrow." He gestured with his hands. "It's going to be really tough to eat at May's after this."

They all laughed.

Chapter 7

A Wrong Is Righted

Luke felt anxious as he drove home. "Lord, please help me to stay calm. I know you have the beginning and the ending of this thing in control. It's us who get uptight and nervous sometimes when waiting. I would stop and see Pastor O'Reilly, but I believe you want me to get home and take care of Aurora." He chuckled. "Lord, I've never really been much for cats, but this one is different. I'm still amazed at her pointing out the car that night. I just wish I had gone after the driver." He shook his head. "No, I did sense not to. If I had gone after her, I may not have been able to answer the call to the manor. It was me who had to be there to formally meet Harold Simpson. We've seen each other at church, but never really talked." He blew out a heavy sigh. "Your wisdom never ceases to astonish me. Thank you, Lord."

He pulled into his driveway, turned off his car, got out, walked up the front steps, and put the key into the lock. When he opened the door, Aurora was sitting on the floor in the hallway. "Okay, girl, how on earth did you get out of my bedroom? I know I closed the door."

He was startled when he heard someone coming down the stairs. "Sorry, Mr. Drake, but I forgot my purse earlier when I stopped by to bring in some detergents and cleaning stuff. I looked high and low for it, and then I remembered I left it here after I put away the stuff." Mrs. Jeffers gestured toward Aurora. "When I went upstairs to the closet where I keep my cleaning stuff and purse, I heard a meow. When I opened your bedroom door, this cat came out. I didn't know what to do. Then I heard you coming in the front door, so I figured you might know."

Luke chuckled. "It's okay, Mrs. Jeffers, she's a good friend of mine." He gazed at her purse. "I see you have your purse. Don't let me keep you. I'm sure you have things to do."

Mrs. Jeffers clenched her jaw. "Will I have to do any cleaning of the litter box? I mean, will the cat be part of my job?"

"Nope, I'll take care of my good friend." He nodded. "You have a good evening."

She hurried out the front door.

Luke picked up Aurora and chuckled. "Well, the town will be gossiping tonight. I'm sure she'll hurry over to the diner to find out what May knows about the cat." Aurora purred while Luke pet her. "Well, my little friend, are you hungry? Let's see what you would like to have. I know the Simpson's said you like milk. If you're not hungry, would you like a nice bowl of milk?"

While Luke was getting Aurora some milk, he heard the front door. May came bursting into the kitchen and gazed at Aurora with eyes blazing. "What's that cat doing here? You never asked my permission to have a cat."

Luke combed back his curls with his right hand. "Who's taking care of the diner?"

"I had Mrs. Jeffers watch it for a bit. She's helped me before." She gestured with her right hand towards Aurora. "The diner is none of your business. I asked you about the cat. What's a black cat doing here?"

"Well, as the diner is none of my business, what business is it of yours what a cat is doing in my house?"

"What's that supposed to mean? I live here too."

"Yes, as my guest."

"Don't get cute with me; I've lived in this house five more years than you. If you remember, I'm older than you."

"How many years in this house is irrelevant. It's the name on the title that counts."

May took on a posture of superiority. "Look, Luke, I'm not staying in a house with a black cat. It will have to go."

"May don't tell me who or what I can have in my house. If you choose not to stay here, that's your business." He gestured with his right hand towards the cat. "It's the Lord who brought me and this cat together, and let me tell you, Aurora is not leaving."

She looked at him with her eyes blazing, turned around, walked out of the house, and slammed the door.

"Whew!" Luke said. "Well, Aurora, I told you to watch out for May." He sat down on a kitchen chair and bowed his head. "Lord, I pray I didn't step out of line, but I felt it's time for Christians to take a stand and not be intimidated. May has sort of ruled me. Of course, I know I've allowed it. I didn't want to upset her, but I know I can't allow it anymore. It seems I've grieved your Holy Spirit by permitting her to stop me from talking about you in my own home. Please give me the wisdom and the strength not to be concerned about anyone or anything more than you. In Jesus name!"

He picked up Aurora. "I think you and I should call it a night. I'm tuckered out. Besides, I can't do anything until after tomorrow night. I think the first thing I'll do in the morning is put a lock on my bedroom door to keep you safe." He let out a heavy sigh. "It's pretty awful when I'm not sure if May would try to get you out of here. When someone doesn't serve the Lord, they can be taken over by the devil at his will. They're helpless against him without Jesus. The seven sons of Sceva sure reveal that."

As he walked toward the stairs, he heard the front door. When he turned around, May was standing there. "Luke, I'm sorry about the spectacle. You're right what you do in your house is your business. You never try to interfere with the diner, and I have no right to do so in your house. I think I forget it's your house, since

I've lived here for thirty-eight years." She gestured at Aurora. "I'll not hurt the stupid cat. I guess I got ticked off by Mrs. Jeffers." She paused. "What did you say her name was?"

"Aurora."

Her eyebrows scrunched together. "Doesn't that have to do with the Northern Lights?"

"Yes, but I also think it has to do with the light she brought to Elizabeth's life. Anyway, it's a lovely name." He smiled at Aurora. "She's a very beautiful little girl."

She gazed at the cat. "Well, Aurora, I may be a witch at times, but I do welcome you into the family." She looked at her watch. "I better get back and get everything closed up for the night."

After she left, Luke went upstairs to his bedroom. He put Aurora down and proceeded to get ready for bed. "Lord, I thank you for the miracle you just performed in May." He stroked his chin with his right thumb and forefinger. "Perhaps, I've stopped you from working in her by letting her control me. Once I stood firm in my faith and belief of what you wanted, you were able to work on her heart. How many times do we Christians think we're keeping the peace when, in fact, we're denying you?" He blew out a heavy sigh. "Thank you, Lord that I don't have to put a lock on my door." As he got into bed, Aurora jumped up on the bed and proceeded to curl up between the pillows. Luke watched her and chuckled. "Well, Aurora, I wish you a good night."

§

When Luke got up in the morning, he smelled coffee brewing. He quickly took his shower, shaved, dressed, retrieved Aurora's food, water bowl, and picked her up to go downstairs. When he walked into the kitchen, May greeted him. "I thought since you're on vacation we could have breakfast together. I brought home some cinnamon buns last night to go with our coffee."

Luke nodded. "Sure, I can have breakfast with you. Just let me give Aurora her breakfast first, and then I'll join you." He gave the cat her food, filled up her water bowl with fresh water, and then sat down. "Is there anything you wanted to talk about?"

"Not really, I just thought it might be nice to have breakfast together. You're usually gone before six and I don't get home at night until after eleven. It seems I'm at the diner from nine in the morning until I get done at night. I'm open from eleven until nine, but it takes so much time after I close to get things done and ready for the next day. If you didn't stop in for supper, we'd never see each other."

Luke poured himself a cup of coffee and took a couple of cinnamon buns. He wasn't sure what was going on with May. All he knew is she's been the gossip queen of Burroughville since she took over the diner after their folks died. At present, he asked the Lord for wisdom and to be led by the Holy Spirit. "Well, it does seem good to be on vacation. I had no idea how worn out I've been."

May rubbed her forehead with her right hand. "I realized all I've done is work the diner since I was eighteen. I've always wanted to see some of the world, but I don't have time to do anything. I'm not sure what happened last night with the cat, but I'm confused about a lot of things." She gestured with her hands. "I don't mean about Aurora, but about me and my life. It's like I want to take a vacation or something, but I can't close down the diner."

"Well, if you would like someone to run it for you, I know the perfect person. I mean, she is someone you could trust. Of course, we'd have to ask her first."

May's eyebrows scrunched together. "Who's that?"

"Margie Cooke."

"You mean Mitchell's wife?" She gave out a heavy sigh. "Aren't they part of that Bible crowd?"

"Yes."

"Look Luke, I may be sitting here having breakfast with you, but I'm not willing to go that far."

Luke grinned. "Well, I was just trying to be helpful. If you want to take a vacation, you have to make sure the person you leave in charge can not only cook but can be trusted."

They had a peaceable breakfast, which was their first breakfast together in about fifteen years. Luke brought up many Bible truths their folks always used to say, and May didn't say anything. After she left, Luke cleared the table and spent time with Aurora. Then he got out his Bible to read. As he sat reading, the front door opened. It was Mrs. Jeffers who starts at ten and works until six. When she entered the kitchen, she gave a slight screech. Mr. Drake are you all right?" She gazed at his Bible. "I thought you would be at work."

"I'm on vacation. You may proceed with your duties." He picked up Aurora, held her in his right arm, and picked up his Bible with his left hand. "I'll just finish my reading upstairs. I wouldn't want to hinder your work."

"Okay, I'll just get my cleaning stuff out of the closet upstairs, and I'll not concern myself with your bedroom or bathroom."

"That will be fine. As a matter of fact, you can leave my room alone until further notice. Since I'm on vacation, I know how to clean it myself." He proceeded upstairs, put Aurora down, and placed his Bible on his desk. As he opened it, he sensed the Lord prompting him to pray. "Lord, something's wrong. Please help me to pray." He paused to listen. "Mrs. Jeffers has been stealing from us. What do you mean? Oh Lord, she's been supplying herself and her daughter with cleaning supplies at our expense." He blew out a heavy sigh. "What do you want me to do?"

Luke got up from his desk and walked downstairs to where Mrs. Jeffers was. "Excuse me, but I would like to see the bills for the cleaning supplies you buy for our house."

The color drained from her face. "What do you mean?"

"You know the receipts for the charges you claim are for the supplies to clean our house and do our laundry."

She started to breathe a little heavy. "I don't keep the receipts. May has never asked for them."

"Well, May won't be handling this anymore, I will. The point, Mrs. Jeffers, is I believe you've been supplying yourself and your daughter with cleaning supplies at our expense for the last eight years. I won't ask you to pay us back, but you'll have to find another job."

She trembled. "How did you find out?" She paused. "It must have been my daughter's ex-husband. He said he'd get even with her for divorcing him." She gestured with her right hand. "My daughter had no choice with his drunken fights all the time."

"All I'll say to you is that you no longer have a job here." He paused. "Please don't give us as a reference, or I'll be forced to tell the truth."

Luke followed her upstairs to retrieve her purse, followed her downstairs, and put out his right hand. "I would like my house keys."

She reached into her pocket, took his keys off her key chain, dropped them on the floor, and stormed out of the house. Luke waited until she was gone and then picked up the keys. "Well, Lord, I'd better tell May about this. I'll just let her know Mrs. Jeffers thinks her ex-son-in-law told me." He hurried back upstairs. "Well, Aurora, it looks like I'll be cleaning until we can find someone to take Mrs. Jeffers's place. I'm sure glad I have six weeks off. Anyway, I better tell May before she hears about it." He gestured to his door. "I won't close the door. You may investigate the house while I'm gone."

§

When Luke pulled up to the diner, he noticed several people were in there. "Well, I can always talk to May in the kitchen." As he walked in, May was coming out with a tray of food. He walked past her into the kitchen.

May soon followed him. "What are you doing here at this time? Is something wrong?"

"I believe a wrong is righted."

May's eyebrows scrunched together. "Something wrong has been righted?"

Luke stroked his chin with his right thumb and forefinger. "It seems Mrs. Jeffers has been using your good heart to keep herself and her daughter supplied with cleaning supplies at our expense for eight years."

May's eyes blazed. "How did you find out? I really trusted her."

"It seems her ex-son-in-law has known it for eight years." He threw up his hands. "I had no choice. She's no longer cleaning house for us. I figured I'll do what I can while on vacation." He paused. "This time, I'll find someone to clean the house."

May rubbed her forehead with her right hand. "All these years, I thought of her as a friend." She sighed. "I've even let her watch the diner several times for me. This is all so shocking. I wonder what she stole from the diner?"

Luke shrugged his shoulders. "I know, I was quite taken aback by it. It just goes to show you may not really know someone." He looked at his watch. "It's only a little after eleven, but I probably should have some lunch." He combed back his curls with his right hand. "I'm feeling rather hungry after that ordeal."

May gave out a heavy sigh. "I know what you mean. Why don't you have a seat and I'll get you some of today's special. It's lasagna, spinach salad, and garlic bread."

Luke took a seat and prayed he wouldn't eat his lunch while comparing it with last night's supper at the Cooke's.

May brought him out his lunch and poured him a coffee. "I also have some freshly baked blueberry pie and vanilla ice cream. That's always been your favorite. Would you like some?"

Luke chuckled. "Since when do I turn down blueberry pie and ice cream?"

May laughed. "I'll get it for you when you're ready."

"Okay." Luke sat there eating and watched some of the town gossips busy eating and tittle-tattling all the while. He heard the name of Elizabeth Johnson mentioned continuously. Yet, May wasn't joining in as usual. He figured she was still in shock about Mrs. Jeffers. When May came out with a tray of food, he nodded his head to her. Within minutes, she brought his pie topped with vanilla ice cream. "I gave you an extra-large helping. I hope it's not too much."

Luke gave a wide grin. "I'll try to force myself."

May laughed and went back into the kitchen.

When Luke finished, he went into the kitchen. "Well, I'm leaving. I'll see you later." He paused. "I figured I'll do some laundry, spend time with Aurora, and then I have some things to do, so I may not make supper."

"Okay, I'll see you here or when I get home."

Luke gave her a kiss on her forehead and left.

§

Luke gave a heavy sigh. "Lord, I felt bad not telling May why I wouldn't be there for supper." His face screwed up. "I know she's friendly, but I still can't trust her. It's best if she doesn't know what I'm doing." When he walked in the front door, there was Aurora waiting for him. He picked her up and she licked his face. "Listen girl, you're getting me too attached to you. Once Elizabeth gets out of jail, you'll have to go back home." He put the cat down. "I have to get some laundry done. You can keep me company. While the laundry's going, I'll finish the kitchen. Mrs. Jeffers started it, but never finished." He looked at his watch. "It's twelve-thirty and I want to be at Pastor O'Reilly's before four. If I leave the parsonage by five, I'll have plenty of time to be at the Cooke's on time." He stroked his chin with his right thumb and forefinger. "Well, Aurora, I never fancied myself as the Clean Right Maid that's advertised all the time." He grabbed his head with both hands. "Wait a minute! I'll ask Pastor O'Reilly if he knows of anyone who needs a job cleaning. I'd prefer helping a Christian in need. Besides, I probably should have taken the reins in my house years ago. Common sense says May would have hired one of the town's top gossip for the job."

Once Luke had finished the kitchen and put away the laundry, he realized he had time to vacuum the parlor, the dining room, and the den. When he finished vacuuming, he took care of Aurora. "Okay, girl, I'll take a quick shower and change my clothes. It's still early, but maybe it's better if I get to Pastor O'Reilly's before four."

Chapter 8

The Illuminating Begins

O n the way to Pastor O'Reilly's, Luke felt he needed to pray. "Lord, I don't know what's going on. But whatever it is, I take authority over it in your name. Please give Pastor O'Reilly words his adversaries can't challenge." When he pulled up to the parsonage, he saw several cars parked in front. "Okay, Lord, grant me the same to quiet whoever is in there." He walked up the front steps and knocked on the door. Pastor O'Reilly quickly opened the door. "Luke, please come in." He nodded toward the kitchen. "There seems to be some unhappy church members. Perhaps, you can help."

As soon as Luke entered the room, he saw May's top gossips all huddled into the kitchen. To his left were Tom and Susan Jeffers, Hedy Brown, Adam and Janice Cochran. To his right were Joe and Carol Jones, Trudy Martin, Bill and Bertha Smith. Luke grinned. "Well, Pastor O'Reilly, it seems like you have a kitchen full. Is this a special meeting? I don't remember hearing about it. I guess it's a good thing I stopped by."

Hedy Brown was the first to speak. "Whatever you're here for, this meeting is none of your concern. May already told us you don't think the witch is guilty. The handwriting is on the wall, and she's guilty as blood."

Luke stroked his chin with his right thumb and forefinger. "Do you mean to tell me you're all here to badger the pastor for being a pastor? He would be derelict in his duty if he didn't try to go after one who has strayed away from the flock. Isn't that what Jesus did?"

Joe Jones rubbed his left temple with the fingers of his left hand. "We just saw it as him taking her side. I mean, after all, she murdered her husband." He paused and looked down at his feet. "It just didn't seem right for our pastor to be visiting her in jail."

Luke gazed into Joe's eyes. "Are you saying a prison ministry is wrong?"

"T-that's not what I meant."

Bertha Smith took on a posture of superiority. "I don't think we appreciate you saying anything. After all, May told us you don't believe Elizabeth Johnson is guilty." She snickered. "How absurd, when you're the one who found the murder weapon in her hands."

Luke combed back his curls with his right hand. "Perhaps you've forgotten I'm a Police Officer. We're taught a person is innocent until proven guilty by a court of law."

The color drained from Hedy Brown's face. "I'll admit I don't like her and never have, but I know what my nephew in Jackton went through a few years ago. He was accused of something he didn't do. The evidence seemed to point to him, but it wasn't him. Everyone was convinced it was an open and shut case." She gestured towards Luke. "I think he's right, we should back off until we see how this thing turns out."

Susan Jeffers handed Luke an envelope. "I hope this straightens everything out between us." She pointed to her husband. "Tom never knew anything and was quite upset when I confessed what happened. We were going to stop by and see you after we left here, but I knew I had to do it now." She choked back tears. "I want you all to know what a hypocrite I am. I've been stealing from the Drakes for eight years. Luke called me on it this morning, and he fired me. Instead of asking for his forgiveness, I stormed out of his house like he was the one who was guilty." She turned towards Pastor O'Reilly. "Tom and I came here to tell you we understand why you visit Elizabeth Johnson. She may have lost her temper, but I've been willingly and knowingly stealing week after week for eight years."

Luke's face screwed up. "Mrs. Jeffers, I truly believe you've repented." He put out his right hand. "Let's shake on our new relationship. I believe I've hired a new lady to do our cleaning. Do you agree?"

She grabbed his hand with both her hands. "Meet the new Mrs. Jeffers. She'll be very grateful to clean for you. If it's all right with you, could I work tomorrow to make up for today?"

Luke chuckled. "I did do some chores today, but I would like the kitchen cabinets cleaned out."

"Believe me, you'll have some real organized cabinets."

At that Tom Jeffers came over and gave Luke a hug. "Luke, we seem to have gone astray from the straight and narrow with listening to this town's gossip and prejudice." He hung his head. "You've lifted my spirit. Susan really needs the job." He clasped his hands together. "I think we'll be leaving." He turned towards the pastor. "Pastor O'Reilly, please forgive our questioning you and your pastoral work. This day has proved how far away from God we've been." He took Susan's right hand, and they both left.

Adam Cochran snickered as he watched the Jeffers's walk out. "I believe we have some real weaklings among us. Well, I for one won't do anything to help a murderess. I hope she rots in jail for what she did."

Hedy Brown eyed him. "Adam, didn't you hear what I said about my nephew? He was pronounced guilty because of erroneous evidence. How can we accuse her without it being proven in a court of law?"

He laughed. "I know your husband doesn't appreciate all your gossip, but I didn't think you were a weakling."

Hedy stood with her hands on her hips. "Well, maybe Mark's right. He's been trying to tell me for years how gossip displeases the Lord." She gestured towards the pastor. "You've been preaching it, and Mark's been trying to get me to see." Her eyes teared. "He told me I was no better than an alcoholic, gambler, pornographer, or drug addict. I was just as addicted to gossip as they are with their drinking, gambling, pornography, and drugs." She shook her head. "I'm so ashamed at some of the things I've repeated that caused division in our church and town." She headed towards the door. "Pastor O'Reilly, thank you for not giving us any itching ears preaching. This is one lady who will no longer be a town gossip."

After she left, Carol Jones looked at the pastor. "I guess I'm following Hedy out. There's no reason for me to be here. When I was a young girl, I got so angry at my boyfriend that I almost killed him. If my brother hadn't stopped me, I would be in prison and not here." She gazed at her husband. "Joe, what do you say?"

"I'm with you. We who live in glass houses have no business throwing stones at anyone."

They weren't out the door, when Trudy Martin spoke up. "I don't know if I like Elizabeth Johnson or not. I've just been following the crowd." She hung her head. "I've never even said a word to her. I see her at services, and she seems to mind her own business." She bit her bottom lip. "It would appear everyone was minding her business instead of their own." She threw up her arms. "Pastor O'Reilly, we need to let you do your job." She waved with her right hand. "I'm out of here. See you in church on Sunday."

Janice Cochran took on a posture of superiority. "All I know is that my husband's right. We've got a lot of weaklings in this church." She gestured towards the pastor. "You have a choice. Either you stop seeing the murdering witch, or we'll resign from the church."

Before the pastor could respond, Bertha Smith joined in. "Amen to that. I'll not let some murderer take precedence over me. It's her or me." She stuck out her chin. "Who do you want in your church? Is it going to be descent law abiding citizens or murderers?"

Luke felt Holy Ghost indignation flow through him. "Do you call a couple who were responsible for the firing of a young black girl because they don't like blacks as law abiding people? Their prejudice stinks to high heaven. The Bible clearly teaches against being a respecter of persons."

Adam Cochran's eyes were glaring. "How dare you accuse us of prejudice, when we heard you chose a black cat to stay in your house over May."

"I didn't cause May to lose her livelihood. That poor girl was trying to take care of her three small children. Her husband left her for someone else. Besides, it may be May's home, but I own the house. I have the right to have whoever or whatever I want in my own house."

Bertha Smith's face turned red. "After all May has done for you, you're disgusting."

Luke stroked his chin with his right thumb and forefinger. "I guess you'll have to enlighten me to all May has done for me."

"She feeds you lunch and supper every day for free."

Luke chuckled. "She's keeping her part of the bargain to our father. If I allow her to stay in my house, she agreed to make sure I have a good lunch and supper." He gestured with his right hand. "Is there something else?"

With her eyes glaring, Bertha took Bill's hand, and they both stormed out of the parsonage.

Luke then turned his attention to the pastor. "I guess the Cochran's are waiting to see if you'll stop going to visit Elizabeth."

Pastor O'Reilly rubbed the back of his neck with his right hand. "Well, Adam and Janice, I accept the resignation of your membership." He paused. "I will not be ruled by your prejudice but by the Holy Ghost in all church matters. I'm sorry you feel the way you do. However, you have a free will to do what you choose. There are no hard feelings, and I'll pray for you both." He put out his right hand. "I think it would be good if we part on a positive note."

They stuck out their chins, snickered, and walked out.

Pastor O'Reilly flopped into a kitchen chair. "Luke, my boy, I can't thank God enough that you came when you did." He took out his handkerchief and wiped sweat from his brow. "I think I need a glass of iced tea. How about you?"

"No, I'm to be at the Cooke's at six, so I don't have much time. I just wanted to see if you had any other news." He chuckled. "It's obvious you do now. You told me God was working on the hearts of some in this town. We just witnessed the beginning of the illumination." He grabbed his head with both hands. "I'm flabbergasted at Hedy Brown. You've no idea how many times I've had to endure May and her in their nightly gossip routine." He paused. "Last night was unreal with May. She apologized to me. Then this morning, she made coffee to have breakfast with me. Earlier, she bent over backwards to be kind to me at the diner." He chuckled. "She's either changing, or she doesn't want me to put her out of the house. Time will tell."

Pastor O'Reilly clasped his hands. "After what I just witnessed in here, I'm believing May is undergoing Holy Ghost conviction."

Luke looked at his watch. "I have fifty minutes to get to the Cooke's. I'm quite anxious to see what Mitchell found out about the license plate number of the Red Toyota. I don't have time to tell you now. But if you're still up when I return, I'll fill you in on everything. I had intended to do it before I went to the Cooke's, but God had other plans."

Pastor O'Reilly smiled. "You can be sure I'll be up when you return."

Luke shook the pastor's right hand. "I'll try not to be too late." He blew out a heavy sigh. "I do hope Mitchell had success."

"Amen! Only God can turn this nightmare around for Elizabeth."

§

Luke was still trying to figure out the change in Hedy Brown and the others as he drove to the Cooke's. "Well, Lord I did say I wanted to help someone in the church who needed the job." He felt his stomach shake with laughter. "You're so awesome. I fired Susan Jeffers this morning and hired a new Susan Jeffers this evening." He yawned. "I do believe I'm getting worn out with all this spiritual warfare." He shook his head. "What I found at the parsonage was quite a shock. How many times does Pastor O'Reilly have to deal with such people? As if he doesn't have enough on his plate, he must deal with such carnality from people claiming to be Christians. Please help him and give him the wisdom to get through all battles."

When Luke pulled up in front of the Cooke's, he remembered the envelope from Mrs. Jeffers. He reached into his pocket and opened it. "Oh my, it's a check for ten thousand dollars. Lord, I didn't realize she stole so much from us." He stroked his chin with his right thumb and forefinger. "They don't have money. What did they do to pay this? Lord, am I supposed to keep it? What do you want me to do with this money?" He bowed his head. "Please give me direction." He grabbed his head with both hands. "Oh Lord, they took out a second mortgage on their house to do this. I know what bank they use. Yes, Lord, I'll pay off the mortgage tomorrow."

Mitchell was waiting on the porch when Luke walked up to the house. "I believe I have some great news for you. Let's get into the house." He looked around and laughed. "Pastor O'Reilly reminded us about the beaver in Narnia, and the trees might be listening."

Margie was standing inside the door. "Yes, let's get into the kitchen. Supper is ready. We'll eat and then discuss the great news."

Luke chuckled. "I'm really hungry tonight. You'll be stunned at what took place at the parsonage before I came here. God is definitely doing some enlightening in this town."

Margie put her hands on her hips. "I guess Mitchell's great news may not be as great as yours."

Luke chuckled. "Let's put it this way, both are the working of the Lord."

Mitchell's eyebrows scrunched together. "Now you have my curiosity peaked. However, Margie will be upset if we allow her cooking to get cold. It's best if we eat and keep our great news for later."

Luke and Mitchell sat down while Margie went to the stove, took out the supper, and placed it on the table. "I hope you like chicken piccata, garlic mashed potatoes, and sautéed summer vegetables topped with Parmesan cheese."

Luke shrugged his shoulders. "I don't think I've had that chicken before. But I have a feeling I'm going to love it, if you made it." He gestured towards Mitchell. "He truly did marry the best cook around."

Margie blushed. "Thank you for the word of praise. However, I've been given the gift from the Lord. Ever since I was a child, it seems I've had the ability to cook."

Luke grinned as he looked at everything. "Well, I guess it's time to enjoy your gift."

Mitchell rubbed his hands together. "That's a great way of saying it." He gestured towards Margie. "You may distribute your gift."

They all enjoyed casual conversation while they ate. After the meal, Margie went to the refrigerator. "Well, I hope you like banana cream pie." She laughed. "It may not seem to go with this meal, but Mitchell has been after me to make one."

"I could eat banana cream pie every day." Mitchell laughed. "However, it might put too much weight on me." He rubbed his stomach. "Margie's cooking keeps this quite content."

Luke sat back in his chair and folded his arms. "Well, I don't know if it goes with the meal or not, but it'll go just fine in my stomach." He pointed towards Mitchell stomach. "Mine has a lot of catching up to do."

They all laughed until their bellies shook.

"Wow!" Luke said. "This has to be the best banana cream pie I've ever had. If I wasn't so full, I would ask for another piece."

Mitchell looked at Margie and nodded. Margie got up from the table and went to the refrigerator. "I felt the Lord wanted me to make two today. When I told Mitchell, he said he wouldn't have a problem eating two pies." She placed it in a container. "This is for you to take home." She placed her hands on her hips. "Of course, there's one stipulation."

Luke's face screwed up. "What do you mean?"

"You'll have to promise to bring the pie pan and container back empty."

Luke chuckled. "I think I can manage that stipulation without any trouble."

"I'll keep it in the refrigerator until you leave." She pointed to the parlor. "I do think we had better get our special messages out."

"Amen to that!" Mitchell said. "I know I have good news, but I'm more intrigued with what news Luke has."

Margie led the way into the parlor, and they all sat down. Luke gestured towards Mitchell. "I really want to hear what you found."

"Okay, the license plate belongs to a Madeline Owens." He handed a piece of paper to Luke. "There's her address." He paused. "Apparently, she's been in trouble with the law before. However, each time, the charges were dropped. It was always some boyfriend. She has a hot temper, and seemed to be in trouble every couple of years. However, but she hasn't been in trouble for over five years."

Luke stroked his chin with his right thumb and forefinger. "That's about how long she was with Barth Johnson." He put up his right hand. "We can't let any of this out. I must pray and see how to handle things. If I make any mistakes, Chief Hopkins will be all over me."

Margie leaned forward. "I know what you mean, but God's grace will guide you. He'll light up your path in this darkness."

"Amen!" Luke said. "He's already been shining light on the darkness." He grabbed his head with both hands. "You'll not believe what happened earlier this evening." He sat back and folded his arms. "First of all, this morning I found out that Susan Jeffers has been stealing from us for eight years."

Both Mitchell and Margie gazed in shock. "What?" Margie said. "She and Tom have been going to our church ever since they were children."

Mitchell gestured with both hands. "Yes, but she's been part of the gossip problem in the town." He shrugged his shoulders. "I don't mean to be talking ill of anyone, but she's also one of those who have earplugs in her ears during the messages." He rubbed his hands together "I've been surprised that Tom didn't see it, but I wasn't going to say anything. I figured the Lord would show him."

Luke threw up both hands. "That's just it. I fired her this morning, she confessed to Tom, confessed her sin to Pastor O'Reilly, Hedy Brown, Adam and Janice Cochran, Joe and Carol Jones, Trudy Martin, Bill and Bertha Smith, and myself." He chuckled. "Earlier, I hired a new Susan Jeffers to clean my house. She told everyone she's a hypocrite who has been stealing from us for eight years."

Margie raised her hands. "Thank you, Lord. What an answer to prayer." Her eyes filled with tears. "You see, we had been best friends up to about ten years ago. She started to drift from the Lord, and I drew closer to him."

"That's not all, Hedy Brown left the parsonage vowing not to be a town gossip any longer. She said her husband implied her addiction to gossip was just as bad as an alcoholic, gambler, pornographer, and drug addict." He paused. "The Lord has overwhelmed me with what he did today. Tom and Susan Jeffers, Hedy Brown, Trudy Martin, and Joe and Carol Jones all repented of their gossip. Pastor O'Reilly told me he was praying for revival, and the Lord confirmed it to me. But to actually see it happening was awesome."

Margie's eyebrows scrunched together. "I thought you mentioned the Cochran's and the Smiths were there too?"

"I did, but they've all left the church. Adam and Janice Cochran have officially resigned. They gave Pastor O'Reilly an ultimatum. He was to stop visiting Elizabeth in jail or they would resign." He shook his head. "It gave the pastor no joy to tell them he would be led by the Holy Spirit in church matters and not them."

Mitchell hung his head. "That does grieve me. You see Adam and I used to be best friends until he married Janice. I've been praying for him." He paused. "God is still able to touch his heart. Of course, he has to be willing to hear from the Lord."

Luke looked at his watch. "Oh my! I promised Pastor O'Reilly I'd stop by after I left here. It's almost eight-thirty. I better leave." He gestured with his right hand. "He said he'll wait up for me."

Margie stood up, went to the kitchen, came back with Luke's pie, and handed it to him. "Here, we don't want the pastor staying up too late. After all, he has a heavy load."

Luke took the pie and turned towards Mitchell. "Thank you for getting me this information. I'm quite excited about the whole thing, but I definitely need prayer to walk circumspectly." He paused, looked at the pie, and gazed at Margie. "Thank you for a delicious meal, great conversation, and this wonderful banana cream pie."

"Godspeed," Mitchell said, as he let Luke out their front door.

"Amen, I'll need to be led by him."

Luke went to his car, put the pie on the floor behind his seat, and sat in the driver's seat. As he started the car, he prayed. "Lord, I want to thank you for all you're doing. Please continue to lead me by your Spirit."

Chapter 9

Revival Comes to Burroughville

As luke pulled up to the parsonage, he saw the lights were still on. He hurried to the door, and it opened before he could knock. "Luke, I've been waiting for you. I have some great news."

Luke followed him into the kitchen. "I see you have the chamomile tea ready." He paused. "I hope I didn't make you wait too long, but I believe I have some great news."

"I was working on a message and didn't even notice the time. Besides desiring to know what you found out, I have some fantastic news to share."

"Do you like banana cream pie?"

The pastor laughed. "It's my favorite. Why do you ask?"

"I seem to have one in my car. Margie gave it to me when I left. I'll be right back."

Luke quickly went to his car, brought in the pie, and placed it on the table. Pastor O'Reilly had plates ready with forks. "I didn't want to waste time, so I got out the plates and forks. Let's have a piece with our tea." He clasped his hands together. "It feels like

Christmas. I haven't had banana cream pie since before my wife died. She always made it for me to have on Sundays after church." He paused. "May I cut it?"

"Of course," Luke laughed. "Just make sure the pieces are big enough. It's quite delicious. Margie is some great cook."

They both had their pie and tea. When they finished, Pastor O'Reilly rubbed the back of his neck with his right hand. "Maybe it's time for me to tell you my news. I've been so excited waiting for you to come." He clasped his hands together. "What would be great news to you?"

"Elizabeth's out of jail."

"Besides Elizabeth. What would be great news to you?"

Luke combed back his black curls with his right hand. "May repented."

Pastor O'Reilly jumped out of his chair. "You have your great news. May came here tonight. Apparently, Hedy had talked to her about what happened earlier. It seems Tom and Susan Jeffers stopped by and told her what occurred. Anyway, they were all singing your praises at how you're a true man of God. May told me she had turned on the Lord, because her parents wouldn't let her date Bob Hopkins. Although she's glad they didn't now. She just wouldn't admit your parents were right about him. He may be the chief of police, but he gets on her nerves with his loudmouth tactics." He paused. "May said she became the gossip queen and loved the attention. When Hedy said she wouldn't be coming to gossip anymore, May was confused. Anyway, she had the dishwasher watch the diner, so she could get something from the house." He gestured with his right hand. "She said she had to get someplace quiet. When she entered the house, she found Aurora waiting in the hall. For the first time in years, she heard the Lord's voice. He asked her why she was kicking against the pricks. She fell to the floor and felt the scales fall from her eyes. It was clear to her what she'd been doing. She called Hedy who agreed to watch the diner, so she could come and talk to me."

Luke sat back with tears filling his eyes. "My God, I can't thank you enough. Thank you, Jesus for this wonderful news." He stood up. "I guess I'd better get to the diner and see what May has for supper." He held his stomach. "I'm so full of banana cream pie I don't know how I'll be able to eat." Luke gestured towards the pie. "How about you finish it and give Margie the pie pan and container?"

Pastor gave a slow grin. "I think I can manage that quite efficiently. However, what did you find out?"

Luke chuckled. "Well, I know who the murderer is, and I need to walk circumspectly to bring it all about. I can't say any more at present until I pray for direction. I'll keep you up-to-date with things."

"Godspeed! May God lighten your path to truth."

§

Luke was thrilled as he drove to the diner. "Lord, do I let May know I talked to Pastor O'Reilly, or should I just see what she does?" He paused. "Yes, Lord. I'll let her get it out. She's been waiting for me." As he pulled up to the diner, he saw May watching out the window. "Well, Lord, my heart is bubbling with excitement. I'm actually happy to see my sister."

When he walked into the diner, May ran to him, and gave him a hug. "I've been waiting for you."

"Well, what did I do to earn a hug from you?" He chuckled. "I haven't been knighted or won any awards."

May started to cry. "I'm just so sorry for the way I've treated you since I was eighteen and especially since our parents died. I think I was angry they died before I could admit to them they were right about Bob Hopkins. I believe I was angry with God because I didn't admit it to them. I just became harder and harder at God, you, and anyone who mentioned the Lord." She sat at a booth, laid her head on her arms, and cried.

Luke touched her right shoulder with his right hand. "Lord, help May to give it all to you. Grant her the peace she needs and help her to be strong in you. In Jesus name, I pray."

May looked up at him. "Luke, how have you put up with me all these years?" She threw up her arms. "I had this dream years ago about being popular and travelling the world. It seems I've allowed the dream to be part of my future. I mistook my sowing discord, anger, and prejudice as being popular. But I never had an opportunity to travel the world." She shook her head. "Mom told me I must be careful about dreams that could ruin the present. She said they need to be washed out to sea like the waves wash sand castles." She grabbed Luke's right hand. "Oh Luke, I've been a monster. How will I ever make it right?"

Luke kissed the top of her head. "You're on the right path. There are others who did as you, but the Lord has gotten a hold of them. You're all a little army against the gossip and prejudice that's ruled this town. God will show you the way." He grinned. "Besides, you have me to help you. I'm quite excited about my sister accompanying me to church." He grabbed his head with both hands. "This has made my day." He took her right hand in his hands. "Do you still hate Elizabeth?"

"No! I don't know what was wrong with me. I don't even know her. I just enjoyed being the gossip queen so much that I didn't give anyone a chance." She stood and placed her hands on her hips. "That all has changed as of tonight." She threw up her hands. "I have to get your supper."

Luke laughed. "I think I'll skip supper tonight. I had supper at the Cooke's with banana cream pie for desert." He gestured with his right hand. "I would like a cup of tea. I know you always serve coffee, but I prefer tea."

May sat back down and laughed until her belly shook. "I've never enjoyed coffee. It was part of my rebellion against our parents. It'll be a pleasure to have a cup of tea with you. I purchased some loose-leaf Chinese tea for Mr. McKenna. He has it every day with his dinner." She went over to get a ceramic tea pot, measured out the tea, and poured hot water into the pot. "I'll let it steep, while I get the teacups." She laughed. "You can't have tea in a coffee mug. That's what Mr. McKenna taught me." She then went to the back room to get two teacups and saucers. Then brought the teapot over to the booth and placed it on the table. "Let's sit here and enjoy our tea." She sat down, poured the tea, and gazed at Luke."

I believe God uses Aurora. When I saw her tonight, something in me just burst into love for the Lord." She sipped her tea. "She's something special."

Luke chuckled. "You've no idea. It's Aurora who pointed out Barth's murderer. Now, May none of this conversation can be repeated. If Chief Hopkins hears any of it, it'll cause a lot of problems for me."

"Believe me with the help of the Lord, I'll be as silent as the grave. I'm truly a changed woman." She hung her head. "Do you know I had the chance to date Nathan O'Connor after Bob Hopkins wanted to date me, and I refused. I was so angry at God that I wanted nothing to do with any Christians. He's not only one of the nicest guys around, but he's a wealthy businessman who travels a lot." She threw up her hands. "I just told you about my dream to travel the world."

"If Nathan was interested, he may still be. Perhaps, that's why he's never married. He may have been praying for the Lord to move on your heart."

May reached across and put her right hand on Luke's left hand. "You may be right. He comes in here every afternoon when he's in town." She pointed to the corner booth. "He sits there, bows his head, and I know he's praying." She laughed. "Well, if he's in town on Sunday, he'll see me in church."

"Anyway, about Aurora. The night Barth was murdered, Aurora ran in front of this red Toyota. The driver came to a screeching halt within yards of my squad car. I didn't know who the cat was at the time, and I thought it was lucky to be alive." He sipped his tea. "The weirdest thing was she sat on top of my squad car, and I must admit it frightened me. When I opened my door, she meowed, jumped off, and ran down an alley between two buildings."

"How do you know it was the murderer?"

"I went to Capital City on Monday and met one of Barth's old army buddies. However, before that, I went to his so-called office building. That's when I found out he lived on the third floor with his girlfriend."

May gasped. "What did you say?"

"That's right. He lived with his girlfriend. I believe she's the murderer, but I must do some further investigating. Mitchell has been helping me with tracking down the license plate number of the red Toyota. I believe I know what she looks like." He stroked his chin with his right thumb and forefinger. "You see, when I was at the Johnson Manor after the murder, this well-dressed, attractive, and very cunning brunette came in. She pretended to be Barth's secretary and tried to kill Elizabeth."

May's eyebrows scrunched together. "How do you know she wasn't his secretary?" She gestured with her right hand. "I mean, he was a wealthy businessman."

"May, it's been all over the news that he was nothing but a gambler and drunk. It was Elizabeth who set him up in the office building and gave him the phony title. However, there was no business going on. Elizabeth was ashamed that she married a non-Christian and made everyone think he had the money."

"I heard the news, but I thought things were mixed up. We were all convinced he was the one with the money."

Luke sipped his tea. "Besides, Wayne Olson told me everything. He's Barth's old army buddy. He said Barth only married Elizabeth for her money. He was in big trouble with some loan sharks for his gambling. If Elizabeth hadn't bailed him out on their honeymoon, he'd have been history. That's when he told her it was her money he loved and not her." He sipped his tea. "Besides, the only reason he came home every other weekend was to get his substantial allowance. He badgered her semi-monthly for more money. She may have done wrong in marrying him, but she wasn't going to give him any more than what was agreed upon." He combed back his curls with his right hand. "I'll give her credit for standing against him all those years." He paused. "I found that out from her butler and his wife. They said he relentlessly plagued her, but she just stood there and took it. She felt it was her fault for marrying him and not seeking the Lord."

May sat back with tears in her eyes. "That poor girl. What this town has put her through." She threw up her hands. "Accusing her of spending her husband's money, when he was spending hers on alcohol, gambling, and a girlfriend. And I encouraged it all. I'm so ashamed." She placed her right hand on his left hand. "How will I ever make everything right?"

"Remember what our parents always said. A baby takes one step at a time. You take one positive step at a time, and the Lord will take care of the rest."

She sipped her tea. "Well, the first thing I want to do is to see if I can visit Elizabeth and ask her for forgiveness. I'll also let her know what a treasure Aurora is. The next thing I'll do is make sure May's Diner is no longer the house of gossip."

"Amen! Now, we need to pray that I can do what is needed without the chief knowing anything." He paused. "If you get to see her, make sure you don't mention anything about this. Ears may be listening and run to tell the chief what you said."

May laughed. "That reminds me of Narnia where the beaver said the trees would be listening."

Luke laughed until his belly shook. "That's what Pastor O'Reilly always says. You really are on the right path." He stood up. "I think Aurora has been alone long enough. I better get home." He gestured with both hands. "Unless you need me to help you close up."

May stood up and shook her head. "No, I'm done for the night. I'll follow you home. I just want to get out of here for a while. It's like I have to sanitize the whole place." She gave a heavy sigh. "Of course, the sanitizing had to start in me. What a strange feeling. I feel free for the first time in years. I just wish I had told our parents they were right."

Luke pointed up. "Did you forget they're part of the cloud of witnesses watching us. I'm sure they watched the rejoicing in heaven that took place when you saw the truth."

"I did forget that." She laughed. "I still have the study Bible Mom gave me on my sixteenth birthday. Of course, it hasn't been used in years. I'll start tonight making sure it becomes very used."

Chapter 10

Truth Unveiled

When Luke and May walked into the house, Aurora was sitting in the hallway waiting for them. Luke picked her up. "Aurora, my girl! Are you ready to eat?" He carried her into the kitchen. "You just sit there, while I get your food."

While he was getting Aurora's food, May sat on the floor next to her. "Aurora, I don't know what you can understand, but God has used you in many ways. It's no wonder Elizabeth is so attached to you. You're an incredible little feline." She whispered. "I've never been one for cats, I always wanted a toy poodle. You see, my dad was allergic to just about any animal." She looked up and saw Luke standing in the doorway.

"I told her the same thing." He chuckled. "Not about Dad being allergic, but that I was never one for cats. She doesn't seem like one. I can't explain it." His face screwed up. "I told her I don't know how I'm going to let her go when Elizabeth gets cleared of this crime." He put her food down and opened the kitchen cabinets. "Do we have any tea? I really feel like another cup of tea would be nice."

May's eyebrows scrunched together. "If I remember, I believe Susan has some green tea. She likes to have it in the afternoon. I think she leaves it in the corner cupboard." May walked over to the cupboard and opened the door. "Yes, here it is. I heard green tea is supposed to be very good for its health benefits." She put a kettle of water on, took out two cups, and put a tea bag in each cup. "I'm not sure if it's as good as the Chinese loose-leaf tea, but we can find out." She laughed. "I don't know why I stopped drinking tea. That's all Mom and I drank." She rubbed her temple with her right hand. "It was part of my rebellion. Now, I don't even know what I was rebelling against. It seems I was angry when they died, because I didn't tell them I loved them. I should have told them how right they were about so many things. I became hard hearted and would hear nothing about the Lord. I guess I blamed him for my rebellion. As I look back now, I had so many opportunities to tell them everything, and I didn't. You see, I knew it was their love that forbade them from allowing me to date Bob Hopkins." She poured the water in their cups. "We'll let this steep for a little while." She stared at her teacup. "Luke, I think I enjoyed being the gossip queen, and I refused to see anything else."

As they were talking, Aurora jumped onto Luke's lap. "This is what she did when I was visiting with Elizabeth's butler and his wife. They were shocked." He pet Aurora's back with his right hand. "I was told Barth had done something to her when she was a kitten. After that, she was afraid of men. She would stay in the room with Harold, but she didn't get close. His wife, Sarah, said it was because she sensed a different spirit in me than Barth."

May rubbed her forehead with her right hand. "It's the Spirit I've been fighting all these years. Thank God, he didn't give up on me." May put some honey in their tea. "This is how Mom and I drank our tea." She took a sip. "This is quite nice. I think I'll buy us some green tea tomorrow. No wonder Susan drinks it."

Luke grinned. "I think it's rather refreshing. The honey does make it quite tasty."

They both drank their tea and Luke was the first one to get up. "Well, I think Aurora and I had better get some rest. I have a busy day tomorrow."

May grabbed his right hand with both hands. "Lord, please help my brother to unveil the truth. In my heart, I believe she's innocent. Please lead him to the murderer and get a full confession. In the name of Jesus, I pray."

"Amen! I believe God is in control of it all. All I have to do is be led by his Spirit and all will be fine." He kissed her forehead. "Goodnight, sis." He chuckled. "Now, you're truly a sister in the Lord and my biological sister."

She gave him a hug. "Luke, I feel like I've awakened from a coma or something. All these years I've wasted a special friendship I could've had with you. I'm so sorry."

"I forgive you." He paused. "Besides, this is something I've been praying and praying for. I'm totally elated." He chuckled. "Now, let's hope I can calm down enough to sleep. There's so much to be done tomorrow. I must be alert and on top of it. That Madeline is quite a crafty one. You should have seen how she came into the manor, head held high, blew smoke towards a detective's face, and grabbed Elizabeth by the neck. The chief and I had to pull her off. It was only the grace of God Elizabeth wasn't hurt."

"I'll ask Hedy to pray for you. Don't worry, I won't tell her anything. I'll say you need wisdom, because you believe Elizabeth is innocent." She grinned. "I don't believe Hedy will be a problem. She was quite adamant about not visiting me as long as I was the queen of gossip." She gestured with her right hand. "Well, she didn't actually say that, but I know what she meant."

"Thank you. I'll visit Pastor O'Reilly first thing in the morning to see if he has any news I need be aware of. Then I intend to see Detective Peter Pruitt alone. I know he's trustworthy. He always listens to the pastor's sermons." His face screwed up. "Besides, I've seen his face when the chief makes fun of me." He paused. "He mocked me the night of Barth's death. He told Madeline her boss wouldn't be signing any more papers, unless Officer Drake could use his Bible quotes to raise him from the dead."

"Why did you stay there? I mean, you're telling me he makes fun of you all the time?"

"Yes, but the Lord told me to stay. He said I would make a difference in this town. I just had to wait on him." He blew out a heavy sigh. "I'm not saying it hasn't been a struggle at times, because it's been quite tough."

"Especially with a gossip queen sister who derided you too."

"Okay, enough of that. You've asked God to forgive you, and he has. What God forgives, he forgets. You must start confessing who you are now, and not who you were."

May gave a slow grin. "Yes, I'm now the gossip hater. My only desire now is to please the Lord, and Hedy made it quite clear that gossip displeased God."

§

Luke was up early. "Well, Aurora today is going to be quite a day. I need to walk circumspectly and not give place for any mistakes." He brought her downstairs and was surprised to find May waiting in the kitchen. "You're up early. Is everything all right?"

May laughed. "I thought it would be nice to have breakfast and a cup of tea with you. I made scrambled eggs, home fries, English muffins, and ham." She gestured with her right hand. "Have a seat, and I'll get you a plate." She paused. "Do you want to feed Aurora first?"

Luke put Aurora down. "I brought her food down with me, but I think I'll put her food in the cupboard from now on." He fed Aurora and sat at the table. "Okay, where's my breakfast?"

May placed her hands on her hips. "It's coming right up, sir."

They both laughed as May set their breakfast on the table. "I went to the diner earlier to get the ham, one of the teapots, some loose-leaf tea, teacups, and saucers. I'm going to see about getting some loose-leaf green tea." She paused, poured their tea, and put honey in them. "Anyway, let's eat. I seem to be ravenous." She rubbed her temple with her right hand. "I think I'll finish cooking at the diner and ask Hedy to watch it for a couple hours. I really want to see Elizabeth today. All I could do last night was pray for her." She sighed. "How did she handle all the abuse from this town? As if she wasn't going through enough with a snake of a husband. We were all deceived into thinking she had the model husband." She sipped her tea. "All the time, he was a scoundrel."

Luke swallowed his food. "Believe me, she's living proof of God's grace being sufficient. I've admired her from the start. It was unbelievable to watch her take the abuse from this town and never retaliate." He stroked his chin with his right thumb and forefinger. "I just know I need to see Pastor O'Reilly and then see Pete. He's one detective who will help and not try to get the glory. I don't know how many times he's said if any of the other officers had done what I had, they'd have been made detective by now."

"The more I hear about Bob, I'm so grateful to Mom and Dad for not allowing me to date him." She paused. "Anyway, I'd better get this cleaned up and get to the diner. I want to get everything done as soon as possible. Then I'll give Hedy a call to come and take over for a couple hours." She gave Luke a hug. "I'll see you later. I should be back for lunch, but you probably won't be in town then." She paused. "Prayerfully, I'll see you for supper." She gave him another hug. "Godspeed!"

"The same to you. If I'm done before supper, I'll stop by to see you."

§

On the way to see Pastor O'Reilly, Luke felt a difference in the town. "Lord, a demonic stronghold has been broken in this town. Thank you for what you're doing. Touch Pete's heart to help me." When he pulled up in front of the parsonage, the pastor was standing outside his door. Luke parked his car and hurried to the pastor. "Is something wrong?"

"Nope. I just felt you were on your way, and I was waiting."

"I'm going to seek Pete Pruitt's help. I know he's on shaky ground with the chief and he needs the job, but I know he's devoted to the Lord." He gestured towards the pastor. "I just stopped by to get you up-to-date and to see if you had any news." He grabbed his head with both hands. "What a night I had with May. She has truly changed. I'm still overwhelmed. God is so awesome."

Pastor O'Reilly bowed his head. "Lord, please help Luke in this battle to unveil truth. I know Pete is yours, and we bind the powers of Hell that should try to hinder him from helping Luke. I ask you go before him and prepare the way. Give him wisdom to accomplish what you've called him to do. In Jesus' name. Amen!"

"Amen! I'll head over to see Pete." He chuckled. "I'll leave my car here. I think it'd be quite silly to drive two houses down." As Luke walked down to Pete's house, he prayed. "Lord, please give me the words to say. It's not because he wouldn't want to help, but he has to be more concerned about fighting the darkness than the chief's response."

He blew out a heavy sigh, and rang the doorbell.

When Pete opened the door, his eyebrows scrunched together. "Luke, what are you doing here? I thought you were on vacation."

"I knew today is your day off, and I need your help." Luke followed Pete into his kitchen and saw he and Connie were in the middle of breakfast.

Connie stood up. "Is this police business. Do you want me to leave you alone?"

Luke shook his head. "No, you both eat, and I'll fill Pete in." Luke brought him up-to-date and gestured with both hands. "What do you think? Are you willing to help?"

Pete scratched the back of his head with his right hand. "To be honest, I've been praying for the Lord to reveal what the chief really is. He's made us Christians feel like we're aliens for far too long." He drank down his coffee. "I'm with you all the way. I think it'll be better if we use my detective car. I'll tell the chief I need to do something requiring my car." He looked at his watch. "If all goes well, I'll meet you at the parsonage about nine." He gave out a heavy sigh. "I must admit, it's bothered me about her being in jail. I've never seen her do anything wrong."

Connie gave a heavy sigh. "I'm so pleased that Pete can be of help. I've been so distressed at what this town has done to her."

Pete gave Connie a kiss, and he and Luke walked out his front door. He paused. "I'm not supposed to tell anyone this. Connie and I promised we wouldn't, but I don't think Elizabeth would mind me telling you." He laughed "I mean, after all you have her cat. Anyway, since Connie lost her job because of her illness, we've been in a financial bind. Remember when Connie asked for prayer in church?"

"Yes, I remember, but before anyone could do anything, she gave a praise report at the evening service."

"That's because after the morning service, Elizabeth had secretly handed Connie a note asking us to stay until everyone had left. We then went into the nursery and talked. She asked us how much we needed. We told the amount we needed to catch up with rent, loan payments, etc., she wrote out a check for double. The only stipulation was that we tell no one what took place. We promised. So, you see, I'm more concerned about fighting the darkness surrounding her than anything else."

Luke grabbed his head with both hands. "She's more incredible than I even thought. What a woman of God!"

"She truly is." He paused. "Okay, I'll see you in a bit at the parsonage."

Luke went back to the parsonage and Pastor O'Reilly was watering his plants. "Luke, that was fast."

"Pete has agreed to help me. He's going to meet me here about nine. I'll just sit in my car and pray while I wait." He paused. "Do you need help with anything?"

"I'm just fine. You sit in your car and get direction from the Lord. Besides, I must leave shortly. Today is my prison ministry." He clasped his hands together. "Of course, I'll have to visit Elizabeth, but I won't tell her what's going on. Although God is moving, I don't know who'll head straight to the chief. The Lord wouldn't be pleased if I mess up his plan."

Luke shook his head, opened his door, and sat in the driver's seat. "Oh Lord, I'm excited and anxious at the same time. Please help me to calm my heart and just rest in you. I need your wisdom in fighting the darkness" He sat back in the seat closed his eyes and started to sing all the hymns that came to him. He was startled when his passenger door opened. "Pete, I didn't see you come up."

Pete laughed. "It's no wonder, since you were having church. I could hear you singing as I walked down from my house." He looked around. "Anyway, I told the chief I needed to use my unmarked car to check on a case. He seemed to be off someplace and just nodded his head." He paused. "I'm ready, if you are?"

Luke nodded. "Yes, it'll look more official if we use an unmarked car when we confront Madeline."

"I think you should do the talking. God is leading you in this. I don't want to get in his way."

"That's why I wore a suit today. I wanted to appear like a detective." He got out of his car, put his keys in his pocket, and checked over his notes. "Okay, let's go."

Pete scratched the back of his head with his right hand. "We'll leave town the long way around, so no one sees us together. Then it might be wise for you to drive. I've no idea where we're going."

They both walked to Pete's car, took their seats, buckled up, and Pete sighed. "Well, here we go. May the Lord prosper our journey for his glory!" He gestured with his right hand. "I'm still amazed at the Lord for having Elizabeth's cat run in front of the car. What made you believe the driver of the car was the murderer?"

"I told you, she came to the manor and pretended to be Barth's secretary. Well, her description is the same as what Barth's old army buddy told me." He took out his notes. "When Mitchell looked up the owner of the red Toyota, it's Madeline Owens. She is or was Barth's girlfriend." He paused. "Common sense asks why was she in such a frenzy to get away? Anyway, I trust the Lord to help me handle this."

Pete nodded. "The part that gets me is her trying to kill Elizabeth. She actually tried to strangle her, and the chief let her go?" He paused. "Okay, let's pull over and let you drive from here."

As Luke sat in the driver's seat, he chuckled. "I almost feel like a bona-fide detective today. I'll admit my insides are doing a dance

or something. But at the same time, I'm at peace about everything."
When he pulled up to Madeline's address, he took Pete's left hand.
"Let's pray. Lord, please be my mouth and put the words you want
said to come out. If I miss anything, please show it to Pete. In Jesus'
name, I pray. Amen!"

"Amen!" Pete echoed.

Luke rang the doorbell, and Madeline answered it. "Madeline
Owens?"

"Yes, I'm Madeline Owens. Who are you?"

"We're from the detective division in Burroughville. We have
a few questions to ask you about your former boss."

"I don't know what you're talking about. I don't have a former
boss."

"Madeline, you claimed to be Dorine Morse, his secretary the
night of the murder." He gazed into her eyes. "I'm the one who
took your fake name and address the night of the murder. I don't
forget faces. You're the one who claimed to be his secretary."

"Okay, I wasn't his secretary, I was his fiancé."

"Really, his fiancé, when he had a wife."

She threw up her hands. "Whatever! I don't know! Why are
you here? The murderer is in custody." She stared at Luke. "I remember you, you're the one who found the weapon in her hands.
So, what are you doing here?"

"Because I happen to know who the real murderer is. You see,
when you missed hitting the cat, it was me sitting in the police car
a couple of yards from where you came to a screeching halt."

The color drained from Madeline's face. "What are you talking about? I didn't go there until I bought the papers for Barth to
sign."

"Oh, you mean your red Toyota drives itself?" He pointed to
his notes. "I also have proof you immediately went to Craig's Auto
Rental after the screeching incident to rent the car to come to the
manor with."

Madeline's legs became weak, and she almost fell backwards.
"It was an accident. He was being physical with me, and I grabbed
the thing on the table with my left hand and hit him with it. I didn't

think it was serious, but I did see blood. All I could think of was getting away." She started to cry. "It's all her fault, she was after his money. He was afraid she would take him for everything he had."

Pete jumped in. "Wait a minute! You know you're lying. Don't tell me you haven't heard the news. It's all over the place who the wealthy one is, and that he was a drunk and gambler. It was Elizabeth who gave him a substantial allowance."

She nodded. "But I really believed him. He claimed to love me and not her, but he said she would try to get half. It seems there was a few shaky dealings at present, and he couldn't afford to lose half."

"Well, if you were really trying to defend yourself, why did you leave?"

She sat down on her front step. "I don't know why I did that. I did ask God what has happened to me. Perhaps, if I hadn't, I would have had a better chance with a jury." She put her face in her hands and wept. "It was awful, he treated me like I was an animal and tried to force me to leave. Things were knocked over, I grabbed a hanging rug or something that fell on the floor." She shook her head. "I'd never seen him act vicious before. It was a shock. The only thing I could think about was defending myself."

Luke stroked his chin with his right thumb and forefinger. "Okay, Madeline, I have some praying to do. Since you asked God what's happened to you. Perhaps, it might be helpful for you to seek the Lord." Pete read her the Miranda rights and handcuffed her.

Madeline was put in the back seat with Luke, while Pete drove back. She looked at Luke. "I remember the chief making fun of you and your Bible quotes. When I was young, my mother took me to church." She gestured with her right hand. "However, when I prayed for my mother to be healed, and she died, I gave up on God. You see, I was only twelve with no family. So, I took to the street to survive." Her eyes teared. "I'm not trying to excuse my behavior, but I did have a chance to make another decision. There was this couple in the church who wanted to take me in, but I was so angry at God that I refused them. They lived on the wealthy side of town." She gave out a heavy sigh. "My life would have been so different. You see, my mother tried to encourage me in the right way. She said she was going to be with the Lord, and all her suffering would soon be over. She wanted me to live with the Pringles, because they would be able to give me a better life. All I thought of was my suffering without her. She was all I had in the world."

As Luke listened, he prayed God would give him wisdom in handling things according to the leading of the Holy Spirit. "Well, Madeline, we shall see what the Lord is going to do. You've murdered, whether you felt threatened or not." He paused. "I must admit the thing that bothers me the most was your willingness to let Elizabeth suffer for your crime." He stroked his chin with his right thumb and forefinger. "But I know God is merciful."

Madeline's eyebrows squished together. "Do you know the night I attacked her?'

"Of course, I had to pull you off."

She shook her head. "You don't understand, I could've killed her. But when I looked into her eyes, I saw my mother's blue eyes. Otherwise, I believe I would've killed her." She paused. "That's why I had to get out of there so fast. It was bizarre." She gave a heavy sigh. "I must have been led of the devil. She has my mother's eyes. How could I have tried to kill my mother?" She cried out in a loud voice. "Jesus, please forgive me. I deserve to go to jail, but please let me apologize to Elizabeth." She sat back and just cried.

Pete interrupted. "We're here. Do you want me to bring her in?" He paused. "No, you should do it. I just noticed the reporter from XYZ News is standing outside the station." He gestured towards the reporter. "This has to be God's doing, so the chief can't take credit for this arrest."

Jake the reporter spotted them getting out of the car with a handcuffed Madeline and came right over. "What's this all about?" He signaled to his camera man. "I figure I'll get it on film, just in case it's important."

Luke stood tall. "Whether you deem it important or not, will be your decision." He motioned towards Madeline. "Truth has been unveiled, and this is the murderer of Barth Johnson. She has been read her Miranda rights, and we're on our way into the station to charge her with the murder."

The crowd around was in a frenzy and making telephone calls. However, Jake made sure he was the first to have the official news. "I'll have this on the early news." He paused and put the microphone up to Luke. "Do you have anything else to add?"

"Only this. Justice has been served, and Elizabeth Johnson is not the murderer."

Before he could say anything else, Madeline spoke up. "This may be out-of-order, but I want to say I did kill Barth Johnson in self-defense. I'm only sorry about not confessing it before now."

At that moment, Chief Hopkins came running out. "What's this all about?" He gestured towards Luke. "Since when do you have the authority to do this?"

Luke grinned. "It's not a matter of authority but arresting the real murderer." He paused. "Did you forget I'm officially on this police force? Since when did an officer need authority to make an arrest of a criminal?"

Madeline gave the chief a disgusted gaze. "Perhaps, if you'd have done your job the night of the murder, you would've realized who did it." She paused. "However, you were too anxious to prove his wife did it." She turned toward Jake. "I thought law officials were supposed to be unbiased. This one surely isn't."

The chief's face turned red. "How dare you to talk to me in such a manner." He motioned towards Luke and Pete. "Get her inside and charge her with the murder of Barth Johnson."

As they were taking her in, Mayor Ronald Kingston stopped Luke. "Nice job, Luke. I'll see you later."

§

When Elizabeth was let out, she immediately headed to Luke. "I'm so thankful to the Lord for you." She let out a heavy sigh. "When Harold told me about you and Aurora, I just cried." She put her long blond hair behind her ears with both hands. "How did you know she was the murderer?"

Luke gave a slow grin. "It was Aurora who pointed her out to me. You see, the night of the murder, Madeline almost hit Aurora. She came to a screeching halt just a few yards in front of my squad car. When I realized she was trying to avoid hitting the cat, I just took down her license plate number." He paused. "Can we go to my sister's diner to continue?"

"You mean May's Diner?"

"Yes."

"That would be fine. She came to see me earlier and apologized for being the gossip queen of the town." Her blue eyes sparkled. "May told me Aurora helped her to see the light of truth. Now, she's the town gossip hater."

"We'll have to walk to the church and get my car. Then we'll drive over to the diner." He chuckled. "I hope you don't mind riding in a Saturn Vue, it's not what you're used to being in."

Elizabeth hung her heard. "I guess I've given the wrong impression to a lot of people. My grandmother always said if you can afford the best, you should have it. However, always be mindful of those around you who lack. My self-induced unhappiness caused me to stay to myself." She sighed. "You see, I was so ashamed I married Barth without seeking the Lord, that pride didn't want people to know the truth. Anyway, being in jail opened my eyes to a lot of things. I feel like Joseph. What was meant for evil, God used for good."

When Luke and Elizabeth walked into the diner, May came running over to them. She hugged them both and cried. "Oh Luke, you did it. Thank God for his incredible mercy." She pointed to the corner booth. "Please sit there and let me get a pot of tea." She paused. "Elizabeth, do you drink tea?"

"I only drink tea. I've never cared for coffee."

May laughed. "Well, you two take a seat. I'll get the tea. Would you like today's special with it?"

Luke nodded his head. "I'm quite hungry."

"Me too. I would like a nice meal."

May brought the tea, food for the three of them, and sat next to Luke. "I hope you don't mind me joining you, but I'm really done in."

Elizabeth nodded towards Luke. "I would be pleased to have your sister join us."

They all ate while Luke brought Elizabeth up-to-date with everything. "Anyway, it was Wayne Olson who gave the information needed." He paused. "He wanted me to tell you how sorry he is for not telling you about Barth before you married him." He sipped his tea. "Evidently, Barth had him under some illusion that he owed him his life."

Elizabeth's eyebrows scrunched together. "Whatever for?"

"Barth saved his life when they were in the army together."

Elizabeth put her hair behind her ears with both hands. "I'm too grateful to the Lord for finding the murderer to be negative about Barth. The man was a trial for all those years, but I'll not talk ill about him." She paused. "But who is this Madeline Owens?"

Luke swallowed his food. "She was his girlfriend. He had lied to her about you. She was convinced you were a money hungry witch who would take him for all you could get if he tried to divorce you." He sipped his tea. "The night of the murder, she planned on confronting you. She was tired of being his fiancé and wanted you to know about her. He was furious, tried to force her to leave, became very physical, and she defended herself. She was truly frightened, because she never saw him violent before. During the struggle, she grabbed the bust off the table and hit him with it."

Elizabeth curled her hair around her right forefinger. "That poor girl has been his victim also." She paused and bowed her head. "Lord, whatever you want me to do for this girl, I will. Please lead me by your Holy Spirit." She nodded towards Luke. "I'll definitely find her the best lawyer. Is there a Christian lawyer in this town? I only use my Boston lawyers for business."

Luke combed back his curls with his right hand. "Up to a few days ago, this town didn't have a good Christian lawyer. However, Joe Jones is a changed man." He chuckled. "I think he'll be more than pleased to help you with this. I'll say this for him, he'll be led by the Holy Spirit."

Once they finished eating, Elizabeth broke into tears. "I don't know how to express my gratitude to you. When Pastor O'Reilly told me about you, I did remember seeing you in church, and your being at the Manor that night. But when Harold told me about you and Aurora and how you fed her, I knew everything was going to be fine. I just started to pray for you. I had no idea you would be directed by the Lord to prove my innocence." She paused. "At present, I really need to see my little girl. I've missed her so much." She gazed at Luke. "Could you take me to her?"

Luke grinned. "It'll be my pleasure. She has me around her little paw." He paused. "To be honest, I'm going to miss her. She has me so attached to her." He blew out a heavy sigh. "Let's go see that special little girl."

§

When Luke and Elizabeth entered the house, Aurora was sitting in the hallway. Elizabeth ran over to her, picked her up, and cried. "How's my baby?" Aurora purred and rubbed her face against Elizabeth's face. When Luke went near, Aurora meowed.

"Yes, little one, I've missed you too. My bed is going to be quite lonely without you in it."

While Luke was talking, Susan came out of the kitchen. "Mr. Drake, I didn't even hear you come in." Her eyes bulged and her mouth opened wide. "Elizabeth Johnson!" She paused. "Thank the good Lord. Does this mean you're out of jail?"

Luke chuckled. "Yes, the real murderer was charged earlier. She has confessed and regrets not coming forward earlier."

Susan placed her right hand on Elizabeth's right shoulder. "I'm so sorry for doubting your innocence at first. However, once Luke, who was led by the Holy Spirit, straightened us all out, I felt you were innocent. Once again, I've become the prayer warrior God called me to be. I've spent too many years being a gossip leader. It took Luke being led by God to confront me with my sin to wake me up." She gazed into Elizabeth's eyes. "I do ask your forgiveness."

Elizabeth's eyes teared. "Of course, I forgive you. Believe me, I know we can all do foolish things and find ourselves out of God's will."

Luke interrupted. "Let me go upstairs and gather all Aurora's belongings. I was going to move her food into the cupboard, but now it'll be put back in your cupboard."

"Thank you so much for taking care of her. She's helped me a great deal." She giggled. "I never cared much for cats. But when I found her outside of the office building, she was just about eight weeks old. Apparently, she'd been abandoned. When I looked into her eyes, I heard the Lord tell me she was his gift to me."

Luke nodded and ran upstairs. When he came back down, they went out to his vehicle. He put all Aurora's things in the back, opened the passenger door for Elizabeth who was holding Aurora to get in, and got into the driver's seat. "Well, Aurora, I said you could only stay with me until Elizabeth was home. I'm very thankful she's able to bring you back home." He choked up. "However, I'll miss not seeing you sitting in the hall when I come home." Luke paused. "Whew! I never thought I'd be so attached to a cat."

Chapter 11

Dinner With an Heiress

W hen they pulled up to the manor, Harold came running out. He opened Elizabeth's door. "I heard on the news Luke proved your innocence. They have the guilty person in the pokey." He helped her out of the car. "Sarah and I've been waiting. We're chuffed to bits!" He paused. "We were waiting for you to have tea." He gestured towards Luke. "Officer Drake, would you join us?"

Luke gave a slow grin. "Under one condition. You have to call me Luke."

"Yes, Luke. Now, will you join us for a spot of tea?"

"It would be my pleasure. I sure do enjoy your tea."

Elizabeth's eyebrows scrunched together. "I guess you've had tea with them before?"

Luke chuckled. "Yes, I have. It was the night Aurora jumped into my lap while I was sitting with them." He gestured towards Harold. "He immediately had me see if she would eat. When she did, he was quite pleased and said it would make you rather happy." He looked at Aurora. "Then, when I went to leave, she practically flew into the car and sat on the passenger seat. So, Sarah went back in and came out with the box of her belongings."

As they entered the manor, Elizabeth turned to Luke. "Could I speak with you in private for a few minutes?" She gestured towards Harold. "Please bring the tea into the sitting room for me and Luke."

Harold nodded. "Yes, I'll get it straightaway."

Elizabeth put Aurora down and gestured towards the two chairs where Luke and Harold had sat the night of the murder. "Please take a seat. Harold can put the tea on the table." Aurora loves to be in the Conservatory during the day, and that's where she's headed." She sat down, bowed her head, and then nodded. When she looked up, she gazed into Luke's eyes. "Luke, why did you fight so hard to prove my innocence?"

Luke's face flushed. "I couldn't believe you were guilty. I've watched you all these years. You were amazing. I just admired how you seemed to be above all the gossip and never retaliated. I prayed for you all the time." He blushed. "I asked the Lord to bring a woman of God like you into my life."

Elizabeth giggled. "Well, it would seem he's answered your prayers."

Luke's face screwed up. "Do you mean you'll have dinner with me tonight?"

"Yes, I would be honored to join you for dinner." She giggled. "Will it be at May's Diner?"

"Is that where you would like to go?"

She nodded. "I do believe May and I are kindred spirits." She curled her hair around her right forefinger. "To be honest, I believe the Lord wants us to be better acquainted."

Before they could say anything more, Harold came in with the tea. "Will you be needing anything else?"

Elizabeth shook her head. "Not now. I think we'll just drink our tea. After Luke leaves, I'll rest for a while, and then I'll get ready for a dinner date."

Harold grabbed Luke's right hand in his hands. "Sarah and I knew God had special plans for you in Miss Elizabeth's life." He hurried towards the door and turned back. "I have to give the news to Sarah. She'll be delighted."

Luke and Elizabeth both laughed as Elizabeth poured the tea. "I do believe I feel like a young girl again. My stomach is doing cartwheels with excitement." She paused. "The only thing puzzling me is that when I was young, I believed my husband would be a preacher." She sighed. "I was grieving my grandmother when Barth came in like an angel of light. Now, you're a policeman." She sipped her tea. "Well, I know God is leading this. His Holy Spirit has confirmed it."

When they finished drinking the tea, Luke stood up to leave, went out to his car, sat in the driver seat, and drove home to change into something more casual. May's Diner wasn't a place for a suit. It was pretty good food, but not a formal place.

Susan was still in the kitchen, when he entered. "Mr. Drake, I believe you'll be quite pleased with your kitchen cabinets. There were a few things I didn't know what to do with. They were way up high and looked quite old. I put them on the kitchen table. If you have a few minutes, could you give me some direction?"

Luke gazed at the table. "Well, I'll be. Those things were my mother's. She used them for holidays." He shook his head. "We'll never use them. If you want anything, you can take them. Just give the rest to the thrift store."

She eyed the table. "To be honest, I would like to have them all." She gazed at Luke. "Is that okay?"

Luke chuckled. "I told you to take whatever you want. Take them all." He paused. "Now, if you'll excuse me, I have to shower and change." He gave a slow grin. "It seems I'm having dinner with an heiress."

Susan ran over and gave him a hug. "That has to be the best news I've heard in a long time." She paused. "I mean, outside of Elizabeth being cleared of the murder."

Luke ran upstairs and closed his door. "Oh Lord, I don't know what to say. I'm in awe of your greatness. To think I'm having dinner with Elizabeth is incredible. Only you could have done such a wondrous thing. Thank you." He paused. "I know Madeline is guilty. But I believe you're impressing me that she needs a second chance. Lord, please perform the miracle." As soon as he was done, he hurried downstairs. "Susan, I'll be leaving. I trust you to lock up."

"Sure thing, Mr. Drake. I'm about finished here." Is there anything else you'd like me to do next?"

He shook his head. "I'll have to think about it." He grinned. "At present, I can only think about dinner."

Susan smiled. "I understand. You both have a blessed evening."

Luke hurried to his car and got into the driver's seat. "Lord, I'm not sure if I'm too early. I forgot to ask what time."

As he pulled up to the manor, Harold came out. "Luke, I believe Miss Elizabeth is waiting in the parlor. She didn't rest, but just got ready instead." He paused. "Will you come in? Sarah's eager to see you again. She wanted to see you earlier, but she had to do some things to get Miss Elizabeth's room ready." He threw up his hands. "I pray we get some descent help after this. It has been trying for us with a staff of gossipmongers. Now, it's even more difficult with them all gone."

Luke followed Harold into the kitchen, and Sarah came over to him. "Luke, I'm so glad to see you." She lowered her voice. "I'm delighted you're taking her out to dinner." She laughed. "I don't know who's more thrilled me or her."

Harold interrupted. "I'll tell Miss Elizabeth you're here." He paused. "On second thought, why don't you follow me."

Luke nodded and followed Harold. "I wasn't sure if I was too early." He shrugged his shoulders. "I forgot to ask what time."

As they entered the parlor, Elizabeth was staring at the table that held the Mozart bust. "I hope I get the bust back. I know it's evidence. But it belonged to my grandmother, and I would like it returned."

"I don't see it being a problem. After all, it does belong to you." He paused. "I was troubled why the bust hadn't been tested for finger prints." He threw his hands up. "It was because the chief wanted you to be guilty, and he didn't make sure things were done lawfully." Luke stroked his chin with his right thumb and forefinger. "Perhaps, it's best things weren't done properly." He gave a slow grin. "If he had done things correctly, I probably wouldn't have met Aurora, would not have gone to Capital City, and would not be having dinner with you tonight." He gestured with his right hand towards Elizabeth. "Are you ready to go?"

Elizabeth handed him her car keys. "Only if you'll escort me in your Ferrari."

Luke's face screwed up. "What are you talking about?"

"While I was in prayer, the Lord said to give it to you." She paused. "You see, it's not the car of my choice. It was what Barth always wanted, and I did it to spite him." She hung her head. "I know it was wrong of me, but I guess I wanted to make him uncomfortable somehow. I've asked the Lord to forgive my meanness. You see, my having the top of the line Ferrari, and not him, made him angry. That's one of the reasons he kept pestering me for more money. He asked me to at least buy him one. I refused to give him any more than the agreement on our honeymoon." She sighed. "It was quite an ordeal to have his semi-monthly visits. It was only for money. I offered to give him his allowance at the office, but he said it would cause too many questions. He claimed we had to give some impression of being married."

"Lord, I know this is you. I'll drive the Ferrari, but you know it's not what I choose." He took Elizabeth's right hand. "Let's go have dinner." He chuckled. "I think this might make a stir to some in this town. However, thank God it's not as many as it would have been."

Harold and Sarah followed them out to the car. Luke opened the passenger door, Elizabeth got in, and he got into the driver's seat. "Whew! I must admit this is quite different." He put the key into the ignition and started it up. "Well, here goes."

They made small talk about different things as he drove to the diner. When they arrived, there were more cars than usual outside of May's. "Wow!" Luke said. "I don't remember ever seeing this many cars. I sure hope May's all right." As they entered, there were dozens of eyes on them.

May came right over to them, hugged them, and pointed to the corner booth. "I've reserved your seat." She whispered. "The

Lord told me to reserve it for dinner. It made a few people wait longer than usual, but I wasn't going to rebel against the prompting of the Holy Spirit."

Luke and Elizabeth sat down, and Luke looked around and whispered. "This is amazing. I don't believe Mayor Kingston and his wife, Alice, have been here before." He gestured with his right hand. "In fact, I've not seen most of these here before. God is certainly doing something."

May returned with a pot of tea, two cups, and saucers. "I brought out tea, and I'll bring out dinner shortly. I made chicken piccata, garlic mashed potatoes, and sautéed summer vegetables." She smiled. "For desert, I made blueberry pie that'll be topped with vanilla ice cream."

Elizabeth reached over and touched May's right hand. "I don't know how you knew that's what my grandmother used to make for me. You named everything to the letter."

May's eyes teared. "I heard the Lord tell me to make it for tonight. I must admit I've not made it before." She took a deep breath. "He's so awesome."

While they were eating, Pastor O'Reilly came in. "Luke! Elizabeth! What are you two doing here?" He clasped his hands together. "Of course, you're eating."

Luke's face screwed up. "I usually eat here, but I've never seen you here before."

"I wanted to encourage my new lamb." He grinned. "Besides, I'm tired of cooking for myself. This way I encourage my new lamb and get some good cooking at the same time." He gestured towards Luke. "Do you mind if I sit next to you? This place is packed."

Luke moved over. "Be my guest." He gestured towards Elizabeth. "I'm sure we're both honored to have you sit with us."

When May came out and saw the pastor sitting next to Luke, she almost dropped her tray. "Pastor O'Reilly, what a surprise. Would you like what Luke and Elizabeth are having, or would you like something else?"

He looked at their plates. "Chicken piccata! Oh my, I haven't had that in years. I would definitely like to have the same."

While May was getting the pastor's supper, he touched Luke's right arm. "Luke, it seems as if my congregation is doubling overnight. I won't be able to handle them all. Do you think you would consider being an assistant pastor? After all, you did graduate from Bible College before going to the Police Academy." He gestured with his hands. "I know you have a full-time job, but any time will be so helpful." He rubbed the back of his neck with his right hand. "Besides, my sister on the East Coast died, and I need to be away for about four days. I'll be away from Saturday through Tuesday." He sat back. "I'll need you to give a message for both Sunday services."

Luke almost choked on his food. "I don't know how to preach."

Pastor O'Reilly gazed into his eyes. "Did you forget how you handled the group at the parsonage? You don't learn how to preach, you just let the Lord lead as usual."

Elizabeth reached over and touched Luke's left hand. "You can do all things through Christ which strengthens you."

Luke nodded his head. "The Holy Spirit is urging me to do it."

As soon as Luke agreed to it, the mayor walked over to their table. "Luke, I talked with the town counsel, and they're almost unanimous in this decision. It seems we've demoted Chief Hopkins, who has decided to leave town. He's officially no longer the chief as of four o'clock today." He paused. "What I'm trying to say is we'd like you to be our new Chief of Police."

"Me? I haven't even been a detective yet."

Mayor Kingston gave a slow grin. "I've done some detective work and discovered the chief has been taking credit for your findings for years. I also learned about his ridiculing your faith. I've talked with XYZ News, and they're willing to be on hand at nine tonight for the announcement."

Pastor O'Reilly clasped his hands. "Luke, my boy, I'm so proud of you. It's about time the Chief of Police was a godly man. Now, people will be getting the lawful treatment which has alluded this town."

Luke bowed his head, was silent, and then gazed at the mayor. "This is also the Lord's doing." The mayor put out his right hand, and Luke shook it. "I gladly accept the position."

The mayor nodded his head. "Let me finish my supper, and we'll all convene to my office for the announcement."

Elizabeth touched Luke's left hand with her right hand. "Pastor and Chief of Police within five minutes. I'm so happy for you."

Luke stroked his chin with his right thumb and forefinger. "How about being fiancé in the next few minutes?" He took her right hand. "Will you marry me?"

Elizabeth's eyes filled with tears. "I knew you were going to ask me that. So, I brought something with me." She reached into her purse, pulled out a small box, and handed it to Luke. "It was my grandmother's engagement ring, and it was supposed to be mine."

Luke opened the box and slipped the ring on Elizabeth's finger. "It fits like it was made for you." He paused. "Does this mean you will?"

"Yes. This time it's the Lord." Her blue eyes sparkled. "People are going to talk about our whirlwind courtship, but the Lord wants us to be married on my grandmother's birthday. That's only five weeks away on the eighth of May." She gestured towards Pastor O'Reilly. "It's a good thing you'll be back to marry us."

Pastor O'Reilly gazed at the ring. "My! That diamond looks flawless. It must be about three carats. The sapphires around it are dazzling." He clasped his hands together. "It's set in platinum. What a beautiful ring." He paused. "I do believe I'm as excited about all of this as the both of you. I never had children. Luke has been like a son, and you've been like a daughter." He threw up his hands. "I feel like I'm marrying my children. God is so awesome!"

May came out with the pastor's meal, saw Luke holding Elizabeth's left hand, and examining a ring. "What a beautiful ring." Her eyebrows scrunched together. "Does it mean something?"

Luke gave a slow grin. "It means I'm observing the engagement ring of my fiancé."

May practically screeched. "Luke, I'm so happy for you. I know how much you've admired her." She turned towards Elizabeth.

"This man has been your fiercest advocate. He practically battled the whole town, including me for you."

She gave the pastor his meal, hugged Luke and Elizabeth, and admired the ring. "That ring has to be the most beautiful ring I've ever seen." She gestured towards Luke. "How did you afford such a ring?"

Elizabeth giggled. "It was my grandmother's. She wanted me to have it. I wouldn't use it with Barth. Something inside wanted me to hold onto it." She sighed. "I now know it was the Holy Spirit. It was meant to be for the one God chose to be my husband." She put her hair behind her ears with both hands. "I'm marrying a pastor and the Chief of Police."

May's mouth dropped. "What are you talking about? Pastor and Chief of Police?"

Before Elizabeth could answer, Mayor Kingston nodded his head. "That's right, the City Counsel and I voted him as the new Chief of Police. It'll be made official in my office at nine tonight on XYZ News." He looked around. "You'll have to get someone to take over for you. I'm sure you won't want to miss it."

May looked at the clock. "It's eight, and I believe it's about slowing down for the night. I close at nine, and I know who I can get to finish up for me." She turned to Luke. "What about this pastor thing?"

Pastor O'Reilly spoke up. "It seems Luke is now my assistant pastor. I know he has a full-time job, but he's been such a help to me on several occasions." He clasped his hands together. "As a matter of fact, he'll be giving both messages on Sunday. I have a funeral to go to on the East Coast." He paused. "However, I'll only be gone a few days. Then I'll be preparing to marry them on the eighth of next month."

May gasped. "Next month?"

Elizabeth stood up and took May's right hand. "Would you do me the honor of being my Maid of Honor?"

May's eyes filled with tears. "I can't think of a greater honor." She hugged Elizabeth. "I already love you as a sister. God is so awesome." She threw up her arms. "That's about five weeks. I must get a dress. I really need someone to help me in the diner."

May hadn't noticed the person standing behind during it all until a hand touched her right shoulder. When she turned around, her eyebrows went up. "Nathan! I didn't know you were here."

He smiled. "I just came in a little while ago. Joe Jones told me about what happened in the last few days. I was out of town for several weeks. When I returned this morning, Joe met me at the airport. He felt he had to tell me about everything." He reached for her right hand. "I know I asked you about twenty years ago to date me, but I'm asking again. However, this time I'm going to be bolder." He reached into his pocket with his right hand, pulled out a small box, and took out its contents. "Will you consider marrying me? I think too many years have been wasted, but I believed God would someday touch your heart." He held the ring and gazed into her eyes.

May gasped, grabbed her face with both hands, and cried. "I've asked the Lord to forgive me for turning you down all those years ago, and I accept your proposal with all my heart."

He put the ring on her finger. "If it's all right with you, could we be married on the eighth of May? That was my mother's birthday." He gave a slow grin. "Besides, I have to be in Europe after that for a couple of months. We can make it our honeymoon." He paused. "Is it too soon?"

May grabbed his right hand and squeezed it. "No! It's not too soon." She grabbed her face with both hands. "What am I going to do about the diner?"

Luke interrupted. "You could give it to Margie Cooke. She's a great cook and a faithful Christian."

May nodded. "Yes, I'll do it." She laughed. "I have five weeks to plan for a wedding." She paused and took Elizabeth's right hand. "I would be honored if you'd be my Maid of Honor."

Elizabeth giggled. "Well, we won't have to bother about dresses. We'll both be in our wedding gowns." She grabbed May's right hand. "We'll have to see Jennifer at the Bridal Shoppe in town. I've a feeling she'll be happy to accommodate us."

Luke combed back his curls with his right hand. "Nathan, would it be too much to ask you to be my Best Man?" He chuckled. "Elizabeth and I are getting married the same day."

Nathan gave him a hug. "I've always admired your faith. It would be an honor. He stepped back. "However, there's a stipulation."

Luke's face screwed up. "What do you mean?"

"I'll only do it if you agree to be my Best Man."

Luke chuckled. "It'll be a pleasure." He grabbed his head with both hands. "This has been an incredible day." He stopped and hugged May. "I'm so overjoyed for you." He paused. "I'm sure I'll be moving to the manor, and you'll be moving to his estate on the East Side of town. What will we do with my house?"

Pastor O'Reilly spoke up. "Luke, I don't know if you know it or not, but Pete's house has been sold and they have thirty days to find a place. They didn't have the money or credit to buy it. It seems they had run into some financial problems with Connie's fighting cancer. Anyway, they're the ones who came to my heart."

Luke grabbed the pastor's right hand. "Yes! Thank you, Lord." He looked at the clock and then at Nathan. "We have to get to the mayor's office in twenty minutes. I'm being sworn in as the new Chief of Police at nine."

Nathan gasped. "That's incredible. Bob Hopkins was a disgrace to the position. I don't know what happened, but I thank the Lord." He paused. "May I attend the ceremony?"

Luke chuckled. "You may escort your fiancé. She'll be attending."

May looked around and saw Hedy coming in. "Hedy!" She said. "I need your help."

"Sure, what is it?"

May quickly gave Hedy all the news. "I think that's everything." She grabbed her face with both hands. "Good news is more exciting than negative gossip."

Hedy congratulated them all. "I'll be watching the ceremony on the television." She gestured with her hands. "Two weddings on the same day, this is marvelous news." She glared at Luke. "Chief of

Police and assistant pastor. I'm overwhelmed." She ushered them all out. "You better get to the mayor's office. You don't want to be late. I'll handle things here."

Chapter 12

The God of Second Chances

L uke felt like royalty when he walked into his office the next morning. The first thing on his agenda was to talk to Pete. He told Charles Smith to send Pete to his office as soon as he arrived. Pete no sooner arrived, and Charles sent him to the chief's office. "You asked to see me?"

Luke smiled. "Have a seat. I have something to ask you."

Pete sat, and his eyebrows scrunched together. "Is it about yesterday?"

"Yes and no. You see I'm getting married on the eighth of next month, and it seems I'll be moving into the manor."

Pete jumped up and exclaimed. "You're marrying Elizabeth! God is so awesome. I'm delighted for you." He paused. "I'm sorry, I interrupted you."

Luke chuckled. "It's quite all right. However, I was wondering if you would do me a favor. It seems I'm in need of someone to take my house off my hands. It's yours if you want it."

Pete's eyes bulged. "What about May? Where'll she live?"

"Since she's getting married the same day as me, she'll be moving to the O'Connor Estate with Nathan." He laughed. "After that, they'll be in Europe for a couple of months."

Pete's eyes widened. "I'm in awe of God's greatness." He gazed into Luke's eyes. "Do you know Nathan has been praying and waiting for May all these years?" He threw up his hands. "What will she do with the diner?"

"I believe that Margie Cooke will take it. Of course, I haven't had a chance to talk to her yet. I figured I'll tell Mitchell in a little while." He gestured with his hands. "Well, what about the house? Will you take it off my hands?"

Pete got up and shook Luke's right hand. "You have no idea how grateful Connie and I are for this. I thank God she's fine, but the medical bills about ruined us. Elizabeth helped us with the rent and bills when we had fallen behind. You see, we're in debt over fifty thousand dollars trying to pay the hospital and doctor bills. Our medical plan only covered about half." He sat back in the chair. "I've always loved your house." He gave a slow grin. "Of course the screened in pool and the hedged garden with the gazebo in the middle is so beautiful." He threw up both arms. "Now, it's mine. I can't wait to tell Connie."

Luke grinned. "Go tell her now. Don't worry about the time. As a matter of fact, take the day off."

Pete gave Luke a hug. "Thank you, chief. I never thought I would enjoy calling someone chief, until today."

"On your way out, will you tell Mitchell I would like to see Him?"

"Yes, sir."

Luke was seeking the Lord when Mitchell came in. "Chief, Pete said you wanted to see me."

"Yes, I wanted to run something by you. It seems Nathan and May are getting married the same day as Elizabeth and I."

Mitchell gasped. "Luke, that's wonderful." His eyebrows scrunched together. "Did you say May is marrying Nathan O'Connor?"

Luke grinned. "Yes, I did."

Mitchell sat down. "This is all incredible. Do you know how long Nathan has been praying for May?"

"About twenty years." Luke chuckled. "That's the reason I wanted to speak with you. May won't need the diner anymore. She would like to give it to Margie. Do you think she would want it?"

Mitchell jumped up and grabbed Luke's right hand with both hands. "Luke, you've no idea how often we've wanted to start a diner. Margie will be overwhelmed." He scratched the back of his head with his right hand. "This is an answer to prayer." He took a deep breath. "This is going to be a long day. I could call her, but I really want to tell her in person."

Luke gave a slow grin. "Go tell her now. You can return after lunch."

Mitchell hurried to the door, turned back, and ran to give Luke a hug. "Chief, you're doing a great job."

As Mitchell was leaving, Joe Jones was waiting outside. "Chief Drake, do you have a few minutes?"

Luke nodded. "Of course, come in." He gestured to a chair. "Have a seat."

"Elizabeth came to my office first thing and asked me to represent Madeline Owens. She said we serve a God of second chances and believes Madeline was also Barth's victim." He paused. "Anyway, may I see her?"

"Sure. I was waiting for you. I knew Elizabeth was going to see you first thing. She has a real burden for the girl and wants her to have a fair trial." He stood up. "Well, no sense in my talking, let's go see her. I believe after she gives you the details you'll feel she's a different person." Luke told the officer at the desk what was going on. "Charles, Mr. Jones and I are going to see Madeline. If it's an emergency, you can come and get me. Otherwise, it can wait until I'm through."

"Sure thing, chief. I'll handle things."

Madeline was sitting on her cot up against the wall, eyes closed, and head bowed. When the cell door opened, she was startled. "Officer, I mean, Chief Drake, I was hoping to see you." She paused. "I believe I deserve to be punished, and I was just asking the Lord for the grace to do something good while in prison. He's so good." Her eyes filled with tears." I'm so ashamed of my backsliding. My mother raised me correctly. I'm thankful she never saw what I turned into."

Luke gestured towards Joe. "This is Joe Jones. He's been hired by Elizabeth to defend you."

Madeline eyes widened. "Elizabeth Johnson is paying my lawyer?"

Joe nodded. "She said she wants you to have the best defense possible. I aim to do that." He gestured with his right hand. "You see, Elizabeth believes in the God of second chances."

"I don't deserve a second chance. After all, I almost killed her."

Luke interrupted. "Well, the Lord must want you to have a second chance, or he would not have moved Elizabeth to do it." He shook Joe's hand. "I'll leave you with her. I believe the murder was in self-defense, but she'll explain it to you."

When he returned to his office, Tom and Susan Jeffers were waiting outside his door. "Chief Drake!" Tom said. "We just learned what you did. You're an incredible man of God. We really couldn't afford the second mortgage, but we knew we had to pay you back. Why'd you pay off the loan?"

"When you gave it to me, I prayed. The Lord told me you took out a second mortgage. He asked me to pay it off, so I did."

Susan took his right hand in her hands. "You see, Tom had lost his job. He collected unemployment until it ran out. We were going deeper into debt, so I started to buy our cleaning stuff at your expense. Our daughter was married to a drunk, so I gave her the necessary things she needed at your expense." Her eyes filled with tears. "I know there's no excuse for what I did. It seems once I started, I got farther and farther away from the Lord. Before I knew what happened, I was so backslidden that I used ear plugs to tune out Pastor O'Reilly's sermons to avoid conviction."

Tom interrupted. "I've not been able to find full-time work since, and we just keep going backwards."

They were all startled by a voice behind them. "Would you consider being a chauffeur? I've not had one here, but I'll need one coming up. My fiancé and I will be married on May eighth, and we'll need one." She gave a slow grin towards Luke. "You do agree we'll need one?"

Luke nodded. "Yes, I do."

Tom and Susan both gasped, but it was Tom who spoke. "Luke, I'm so thrilled for you. I thank God for you and your faith." His eyes watered. "It'll be a pleasure to be your chauffer. I'm overwhelmed."

The color drained from Susan's face. "Will May still need me to clean the house?"

Luke shook his head. "No, May is marrying Nathan O'Connor on the same day."

Tom rubbed Susan's back. "I'm sure things will be fine. After all, I'm a chauffeur for the Johnson, I mean, the soon to be, Drake Manor."

Elizabeth smiled. "Susan, we'll need a house maid at the manor. Do you think you could fill the position?"

Susan hugged Elizabeth. "Yes, I sure can." She paused. "Do you need anyone to do laundry? My daughter could use the job. She's divorced from the drunk, and things have been tough."

"As a matter of fact, I will need someone to do the laundry. What's your daughter's name?"

"It's Tabitha Morgan."

"Okay, Harold, my butler, will see to all the necessary uniforms. His wife will give you the schedule." She gestured towards Tom. "You'll have two days a week off." She grinned. "I'll be sure to tell Sarah to give the same days off to Susan." Her eyebrows scrunched together. "There are quarters for the chauffeur. Would you both consider occupying them?"

Susan gasped. "Yes, we would. Our daughter and our three grandsons are living with us at present. This way, she could have the house. It's been quite cramped with only three bedrooms. It's just five rooms and one bathroom." She gave Elizabeth an almost bear hug. "You are an incredible woman of God." She threw up her hands. "No wonder God brought you two together."

Elizabeth put her hair behind her ears with both hands. "If your daughter has three children, how will she be able to work for us?"

Susan gave a slow grin. "It's not only our daughter who lives with us, but her widowed mother-in-law. Grace is a true woman of God. She wasn't too happy when she found out what we did. Now, she can have her own room. Our three grandsons can share our room. It's the largest of the bedrooms, and Grace and Tabitha can choose what room they want." She paused. "What I'm trying to say is that Grace will watch the children."

Elizabeth nodded. "Okay, I would like you to move in this weekend. We only have about five weeks until the wedding. The more I can get settled, the better." She paused. "Luke, Pastor O'Reilly said if you need any of his Bible commentaries to prepare the messages for Sunday, you're welcome to use whatever."

Tom and Susan both gazed at each other. "What messages?" Tom asked.

Elizabeth giggled. "It seems Chief Drake is also Pastor Luke. Pastor O'Reilly has asked him to be assistant pastor. His congregation has doubled, and he needs the help." She gestured towards Luke with her right hand. "Pastor Luke has agreed. He'll be preaching his first two messages on Sunday."

Luke interrupted. "You see, Pastor O'Reilly's sister died, and he has to be away from Saturday until next Tuesday."

Susan gave Luke a bear hug. "This is just getting more thrilling. I'm really looking forward to hearing what you have to say. After the way you handled us during the meeting at the parsonage, I know God will give you something." She laughed. "Believe me, I'll not be wearing ear plugs."

While Tom and Susan were leaving, Joe came back to Luke's office. "Chief Drake, I believe you and Elizabeth are correct." He nodded his head toward Elizabeth. "The girl has had a difficult time of it. It's like she was also his victim." He gave out a heavy sigh. "I've got my work cut out for me. Adam Cochran is the prosecuting attorney, and he's going to fight us all the way. I tried to talk to him after he and Janice left the parsonage that day, and he would hear none of it." He gestured with both hands. "He's out for revenge after what happened and will fight anything we try to do. His heart has become extremely hard. I know it's Janice who instigates him." He paused. "You see, I know before he married her, he served the Lord." He shook his head. "We were still friends until a few days ago. Now, it seems as if I don't even know who he is."

Elizabeth gestured towards Luke with her right hand. "I forgot to tell you I called Martin Phillips and told him I'm selling the office building. He'll be coming to work for us at the manor as our handy man. He'll also be helping Susan with the cleaning." She smiled. "Oh yes, I do believe I heard about the Cunningham's selling their estate. I keep thinking it's meant for Mitchell and Margie." She handed him a signed check. "I believe you'll need this today."

Luke nodded his head. "I just found out that Pete is in debt about fifty thousand dollars from loans."

Elizabeth looked at Joe. "I'll need you to take care of Pete's debt as well as the Cunningham Estate for Mitchell and Margie." She turned her attention toward Luke. "At present, I have to get some paperwork together for Joe. I'll have him bring them into you to sign when everything is completed. I'm putting you as equal partner in all my affairs. There's something else I'm planning, but it'll have to wait until Madeline's trial is over." She touched Luke's right arm with her right hand, and then left.

She no sooner left, when Mitchell and Margie came in. Margie hurried over to give Luke a hug. "Chief Drake, you're an incredible man of God. He's used you in answering a prayer and desire of my heart." She gestured towards Mitchell. "We get by, but I wanted to own a diner. I felt God gave me the gift of cooking for it to be enjoyed by others." She paused. "We stopped by to see May, and she said Joe would handle all the necessary paperwork. She and I are going to the bank this afternoon for her to close out her diner account and open one in my name as the new owner." Her eyes filled with tears. "She's putting one hundred thousand dollars into the account. She doesn't want me struggling with bills. Although she doesn't believe I'll have any lack of customers, she wants to make sure I'm as established as your parents left her." Her eyes filled with tears. "I'm to take it over on Monday. May will work with me the next couple of days to bring me up-to-date with her suppliers and all. As far as the menu, she said it's easier to plan it for the month." She gave Luke another hug. "I'm so excited. I feel like a schoolgirl who just aced her test." She threw up her hands. "I'm just in awe of God's goodness."

Mitchel interrupted. "This is going to be great. I'll get to have Margie's cooking for lunch. No more packed lunch." He rubbed his hands together. "God is so good."

Margie grinned. "The only thing is the diner will only be open from 2:00 until 5:00 on Sunday for the church crowd to eat. I figure I'll see if Trudy Martin will run it on Saturday and then Sunday afternoon." She grinned. "Besides, she's a pretty good cook, and I really want someone who can cook, if needed." She paused. "I'll do the essential cooking for Saturday and Sunday on Friday. That way Mitchel and I can have the weekend. Also, I believe I know who will work the weekdays from supper until closing." She grinned. "That way, Mitchell and I'll eat supper and go home. She looked at the clock. "I really must get back to the diner."

Luke combed back his curls with his right hand. "I guess you have it all planned. I don't know why May didn't do something similar." He paused. "Perhaps it's good she didn't. I think she had to get so worn down for the Lord to speak to her." He threw up his hands. "Anyway, I'm so grateful to the Lord for all of this."

Joe touched Margie's right arm. "Tell May I'll have all the necessary paperwork done asap. I already have my secretary working on them."

Luke looked at Joe and then to Mitchell and Margie. "Mitchell, are you aware of the Cunningham Estate?"

"Yes, they're part of those exiting the town since the revival." His eyebrows scrunched together. "Why do you ask?"

"Well, it seems Joe's office will be purchasing it for you both today. I believe he'll have someone bring the necessary papers for you to sign to the diner."

Margie grabbed her face with both hands. "Luke, you really mean it?'

Luke chuckled. "Yes. Elizabeth informed me a little bit ago about the sale. She believed the Lord impressed it was yours."

Mitchell held back tears. "This is all too much." He laughed. "Don't get me wrong, we gladly accept it." He rubbed his hands together. "Praise the Lord! Wow! To own a diner and now to own such a house. It's situated on about ten acres with an indoor pool, a tennis court, and I don't know what else." He grabbed his face with both hands. "What will we do with our house? I mean, there must be someone who we can bless with it."

Joe's eyebrows scrunched together. "Do you know Benjamin and Martha Pickett from church?"

Luke nodded. "I do. He teaches teen Sunday School, and she works in the nursery." He chuckled. "Their oldest son is only six and acts about thirty. He's so well-behaved." He paused. "Why do you ask?"

"Well, he lost his job when the company he worked for moved to China. He's been working at a place for less than half of what he was making. Anyway, with a wife and three children, a car payment, he couldn't keep up the mortgage. I've been his lawyer for several years and know the situation. Anyway, they're living in an efficiency apartment in Harrington."

Mitchell shook his head. "Does he work there? That's two hours away."

"No, he works at the Mercantile Bank here in town."

Margie looked at Mitchell. "Well, Mitchell, I know who gets our house. You can take care of it. I have to get back to the diner." She gave Mitchell a kiss. "I just hope I can keep my mind on what I have to do at the diner." She exhaled. "Whew! I'm beside myself with joy." She paused. "I have to stay calm and do first things first. I must learn the ropes of the diner, and then I can think of my new home."

Luke gave a quizzical look. "Okay, I believe the Lord wants Ben and Martha to have their car paid off, an income increase, and we'll have them stay at the Clarence Hotel until they can move into their house." He paused. "At present, I have something to do before lunch, but I'll see about Ben and Martha after I speak with

Elizabeth." He chuckled. "Well, I think before Mitchell goes back to the diner, he'll have to come with me to the Mercedes of Burroughville and pick out your new Mercedes. You can't drive up to that house in a Honda Civic."

Mitchell grabbed Luke and gave him a bear hug. "You've no idea how much I love the Mercedes SUV."

"I'll go with you, talk to the manager, and leave you a blank check." He pointed with his right forefinger. "You make sure it's the one you want. Don't look at prices." He paused. "Oh yes, make sure you have the best warranties."

Margie laughed. "Well, Mitchell, I have to get back to the diner. You can show me the vehicle after at the diner."

When Margie left, Joe nodded towards Luke. "I'll get Teresa on the sale of the Cunningham Estate. It should only be a few hours, and I'll send her to the diner for Mitchell and Margie to sign the necessary papers. Also, I'll stop by the bank and tell Ben what's going on. As soon as we can, we'll get Mitchell's house over to the Pickett's." He rubbed his temple with the fingers of his left hand. "At present, I have to get to my office and start the defense for Madeline. I've a feeling Adam will be looking to get on with the trial as quickly as possible. He's still fuming about what happened at the parsonage." He paused. "But I believe God is in on this. Adam is going to find himself kicking against the pricks. I almost feel sorry for him."

Luke chuckled. "Perhaps this will be God's way of giving him his Damascus Road experience. Either way, I believe the jury will have compassion on Madeline. Elizabeth intends to be there to encourage her, and make known she believes Madeline's self-defense confession."

Joe grinned. "I believe the testimony of Wayne Olson is the only witness I'll need." He gestured with his right hand. "Of course, Elizabeth said if her testimony is needed, she's not hiding the truth anymore."

Luke looked at the clock. "It's time for me to get going. I know you're busy, so I won't keep you any longer. However, if you have time to join me for lunch, you're more than welcome."

"That might be a good idea. First, I'll take a quick run into the bank to see Ben, then I'll stop by the office. My secretary should have all the paperwork for May and Margie ready. That way I can take care of this hunger and some business at the same time." He paused. "I'll meet you at May's Diner." He laughed. "I should say Margie's Diner. It was May's idea to change the name. She wants the past behind her."

Luke grinned and addressed the officer at the desk. "Charles, I have an errand to run with Mitchell, but I'll be at the diner for lunch. If there's an emergency, you know where to reach me."

Charles nodded. "Sure thing, Chief."

Chapter 13

Transformations

Luke was relieved to make it through his first Sunday of sermons. Joe was the first to thank him. "Well, during the week I call you Chief Drake and on Sunday I call you Pastor Luke." He nodded his head. "Seriously though, you really spoke to my heart with those messages. It's funny how we can be in church for years and never realize the sacrifice Jesus made. We always think about the cross, but we tend to ignore he was in heaven and worshipped constantly. To think he left heaven to save me is overwhelming. I just thank him I turned back to the truth before your messages today." He paused. "Oh yes, I believe Adam is going to set up Madeline's trial this coming week. He's convinced it's open and shut." He gestured with his right hand. "Praise God I know where I'm going with it all. I'm confident she'll win the hearts of the jury."

As he was finishing, Elizabeth, May, and Nathan came over to Luke. May gave him a big hug. "My brother the preacher. I'm so proud of you." She gazed into his eyes. "Thank you for not giving up on me."

Before Luke could respond, Nathan grabbed Luke's right hand with both his hands and shook it. "I do believe Pastor O'Reilly knew what he was doing when he asked you to help. You and he are one in the spirit. I truly enjoyed both sermons." He paused. "Well, Luke, I think I would like you and Elizabeth to join May and I at my estate for a little brunch."

Elizabeth nodded. "It's fine with me if Luke is willing."

Luke chuckled. "It's fine with me. I've always wanted to see your estate." He paused. "I never knew the Vandenberg's who owned it before you purchased it. They were an older couple who acted like aristocracy, wanted nothing to do with shop owners, and didn't go to church."

Nathan nodded his head. "They were rather patronizing." He laughed. "It was perfect timing for me to buy it. I've been waiting for my wife to move in." He smiled at May. "It was a wait, but worth every bit of it."

May's eyes filled with tears. "I'm so overwhelmed at God's goodness. How could I have fought against the pricks all this time? Stubbornness is not a virtue, but I pray I have the same stamina to fight with the Lord."

Elizabeth smiled. "I believe we've all had some wonderful transformations in our lives. Thank God for his love and mercy."

Luke was suddenly overcome by almost the whole congregation thanking him for his sermons. Even Hedy Brown gave him a hug. "Pastor Luke, you're truly a man of God. I'm so thankful to be back on the right path, so I could enjoy your messages."

§

Luke was exhausted by the time they arrived at Nathan's estate. "Please don't be offended, but I think I need to get some rest. I must be at the station earlier tomorrow. There's so many things to be straightened out that Bob left undone or in a mess."

Elizabeth touched his right arm. "It's okay. Let me take you home. I'll have Harold follow me in the Saturn and I'll leave your Ferrari." She paused. "I'll leave the keys under the mat at your front door."

Luke gave his apologies. "I do hope I'll have another chance."

Nathan laughed. "I think I'll have you both back Saturday for a cookout. Is that acceptable?"

Luke and Elizabeth both nodded. Luke shook Nathan's hand. "Thank you." He grinned. "Then I'll be able to get a tour of this magnificent place."

Nathan touched Luke's shoulder. "Too bad you both couldn't join us in Europe for a honeymoon, but you just became Chief of Police."

Everyone gave hugs and Luke and Elizabeth left. On the way, Elizabeth touched Luke's left arm. "Luke, I think after we're married, you'll have your hands full with our business affairs. There's a lot to do." She paused. "Besides, if you're to help Pastor O'Reilly, you'll be too overwhelmed." Her eyebrows scrunched together. "To be honest, I don't' believe the Lord wants us taking a honeymoon."

Luke nodded his head. "I feel the same way. It's as if we'll have too much to do. Perhaps, the Lord will have us do something at a later date, but I believe we're to get our house staffed." He yawned. "Also, about the job and my future responsibilities, I've been thinking the same thing. Once you told me I would be half owner of everything, I figured it would involve a lot." He paused. "Don't mention this to anyone, but I intend to talk to Mayor Kingston tomorrow. I believe Pete Pruitt is the man to be chief." He gave out a heavy sigh. "Let's pray the mayor sees it the same way."

Elizabeth nodded her head. "Well, he certainly enjoyed your messages today. He may see your need to be in the pulpit is greater than in the chief's seat."

"I pray so." He combed back his curls with his right hand. "You're okay that I couldn't stay at Nathan's?"

She squeezed his left arm. "Of course! To be honest, I'm tired myself. May and I must get our wedding dresses tomorrow. I pray we can get what we want without too many alterations. We both want to get everything settled this week." She giggled. "And just spend the next few weeks making sure everything is settled."

Elizabeth touched Luke's left arm. "We're here." Luke got out of the car. Before he closed the door, Elizabeth said, "I'll see you tomorrow. The Lord watch between us while we are absent from each other."

"Amen!"

As Luke was unlocking the front door, Nathan pulled up, got out of his car, and went around to the passenger side to help May out. Luke went to see May. "Are you okay?"

Nathan nodded his head. "It didn't seem proper for us to be alone at the house. You see, I give everyone Sunday and Monday off. I like a full staff the rest of the time when I'm home." He gave May a hug. "I'll see you tomorrow."

May smiled. "Thank God tomorrow is my last day at the diner. Margie is the official owner tomorrow, and the new sign will be there about noon." She paused. "But I said I would work with her on the books, orders, and things. I want to make sure she understands it all."

Nathan shook Luke's hand, touched May's right arm, and got into the driver's seat of his Cadillac Escalade."

As he drove away, May and Luke headed towards the house. Luke opened the door, and they both walked into the hallway. May shut the door and started to cry. "Do you realize in a few weeks, I'll be in Europe as Mrs. Nathan O'Connor? I'll never live in this house again." She sighed. "I hope you and Elizabeth can join us in Europe."

"Elizabeth and I discussed it, but we feel the Lord wants us to stay here. There's so much that needs to be done." He paused. "To be honest, we have no desire to go anyplace. The Lord has overwhelmed us with his goodness." He gave her a hug and yawned. "I'm going to bed. I'll see you tomorrow." He kissed her forehead and went upstairs."

§

Luke straightened out what he could at the station and headed to see Mayor Ronald Kingston. He was relieved when he found the mayor willing to see him. "Luke, come on in. How's the job going?"

Luke gave a slow grin. "That's what I want to talk to you about. It seems once Elizabeth and I are married I'll have quite a bit to do with all the business dealings. Plus, helping Pastor O'Reilly." He stroked his chin with his right thumb and forefinger. "What I'm trying to say is I'm going to have to quit the police. I believe the Lord would rather have me in the pulpit than in the chief's chair."

The mayor sat back in his chair and stared off. "I must admit I enjoyed your messages yesterday." He pat his lips with his right forefinger. "However, we need a godly man sitting in the chief's seat."

"Exactly! That's why I believe Pete Pruitt is the man for the job. He was willing to put his job on the line to help me arrest Madeline." He gestured with his right hand. "That speaks volumes for Pete's character. He's been faithful to the Lord ever since I can remember."

The mayor laughed. "You're right. He's the one who told me what Bob did against you because of your faith." He paused. "Pete may do justice to the job." He pat his lips with his right forefinger. "I have a meeting with the Town Counsel in about an hour. Once I tell them about Pete, I believe we can get the votes to make him our next Chief of Police." He paused. "I should know by noon. I'll stop by the station to let you know what the outcome was."

Luke shook his hand. "Thanks a lot. I really appreciate this." He paused. "I won't say anything to Pete. I'll wait for you." He chuckled. "This town sure is getting a shake-up from the Lord."

Mayor Kingston sat back and folded his arms. "Thank God for that. The City Council only has a couple of members the shake-up didn't affect." He paused. "That's why I don't see any problem about Pete."

"I better get back to the station." Luke chuckled. "Even if today is my last day, I want to do a thorough job."

"Yes, your principles are why we chose you. However, I can see those same values in Pete." His phone rang. "I'll see you around noon. I have to answer this call."

§

Luke was enthused as he entered his office. "Lord, please let the council agree to putting Pete in that chair."

As he was praying, Elizabeth came to the door. "Luke, it seems Adam has already set up everything and intends to start the trial next week." She paused. "I didn't know things could be done that fast." She put her hair behind her ears with both hands. "He's convinced he has it in the bag. My prayer is that God is doing this, so it can be over before our wedding." She gave a heavy sigh. "Joe has decided my testimony will really touch the jury who were convinced Barth had the money. Then backed up with Wayne's, he's certain the jury will believe Madeline's testimony of self-defense."

"I've talked to Mayor Kingston, and he's probably in a council meeting at present." He paused and made sure no one was near his door. "He's going to see about making Pete Pruitt the next Chief of Police. That's what I was praying when you came in." He gave a slow grin. "I told him it would be too much for me to do our business, help pastor, and be chief. In order for me to continue to help Pastor O'Reilly, I need to quit the police."

Elizabeth gave him a hug. "I do pray he's able to do it. You'll see what I mean. There are times we'll have to fly there to handle things with the lawyers." She sighed. "It's been business that's helped me keep my mind off everything else." She giggled. "Now, business will be like taking vacations with my husband."

Luke kissed her forehead. "I can't stop thanking the Lord for this. It's like I entered a wonderful dream, but I know it's reality. All the time I was admiring you for the way you could rise above all the gossip, God was filling my heart with love for you."

Elizabeth smiled. "I do love you. Although it's only been a short time, it seems as if I've known you all my life. Our spirits are already knit together. That's how it should be in the Lord. I surely know the difference." She paused. "I have to meet May. We have a lot to get done." She twirled her hair with her right forefinger. "Luke, I think you should know we're worth more than twenty billion dollars which includes investments, property, and businesses in the United States, Canada, and in Europe." She paused. "I know I don't live like I'm worth that much. But I felt the Lord wanted me to be comfortable and do for others. After I married Barth, I just stopped doing much of anything and the money just multiplied. I centered upon my sin and forgot I was created in Christ Jesus to do good works." She let out a heavy sigh. "Well, everything has changed. Once we're married, we'll be the helping hands of the Lord doing good to the family of God."

While they were talking, Mayor Ronald Kingston came to the door. "Luke are you busy?"

Luke shook his head. "Elizabeth was just leaving." He gestured with his right hand. "Please come in."

The mayor motioned towards Elizabeth. "It's a pleasure to see you again." He nodded towards Luke. "I have some good news."

Elizabeth gasped. "The council agreed!"

Mayor Kingston grinned. "Yes, they did. As a matter of fact, XYZ News will be here in about twenty minutes. I think we had better tell Pete before they get here."

Elizabeth nodded her head. "Yes, and I have to meet May. So, I'll let you both be about your business." She touched Luke's right arm. "I'll see you later."

Luke threw up both hands. "I think Connie should be here. Pete will definitely want her here."

"She's outside your office waiting for us to tell Pete." He gave a wide grin. "I know it's out of the ordinary for the wife to know about her husband's promotion before him, but I stopped by to get her on the way here." He paused. "I think I hear Jake. They're already here."

Luke got up from his seat and quickly left the office. When he found Pete, he took him aside. "Pete, I don't know how to break this to you, but the XYZ News is here."

Pete's eyebrows scrunched together. "What are you talking about?"

Luke grinned. "They're here to see the mayor swear you in as the next Chief of Police. You see, I'm quitting. I'll explain it all later. Right now, you have to get to my office."

"Wow! I need to tell Connie."

Luke chuckled. "She's waiting in my office for you. It seems that Ronald picked her up on his way here. He had a council meeting earlier, and they voted you in."

As they walked to Luke's office, the cameras were flashing. Connie ran to Pete and hugged him. "God told you to help Luke. You faced your fear of Bob firing you. Now, you're chief."

Mayor Ronald Kingston shook Pete's right hand. "Well, Pete, are you ready to be sworn in as the next chief?"

Pete's eyes filled with tears. "I'm just overwhelmed. This is so wonderful." He sighed. "Yes. Yes, I'm ready."

Luke gave Pete a hug. "I'm so happy for you." He lowered his voice. "May and I are just taking our personal belongings. May is putting hers at Nathan's, and I'm putting mine at the manor. We'll both stay at the Clarence Hotel until our weddings." He paused. "What I'm saying is that you and Connie can start moving in tomorrow. Whatever you don't want of our furniture, you can donate to charity."

Before Pete could respond, the mayor grabbed his right arm. "Okay, let's get this thing done." He gestured with his right hand. "The council members are here."

After Pete was sworn in, Luke pointed to the chair. "Well, chief, I think you should let Jake take a picture of you in your seat." He gestured with his right hand. "I'll clear my stuff out after the picture." He chuckled. "I really didn't have time to put much of anything in the desk."

Pete sat in the seat and smiled for Jake. "I'm still trying to digest all of this. I had no idea any of this was going to happen." He scratched the back of his head with his right hand. "God is so awesome." He got up and grabbed Luke's right hand. "Are you serious about us moving in tomorrow? What about the legal side of it?"

"Joe has the papers ready for you to sign in his office. I've done my part. I signed the house over to you. It's all legal. You and Connie must go to Joe's office and sign a few things. I'll watch the office, while you and she take care of it. When you get back, I'm going to have lunch at Margie's Diner."

Chapter 14

New Beginnings

Adam Cochran seemed to make Madeline's case the trial of the century. It was like he was prosecuting Luke and Elizabeth. Luke wasn't ignorant of his implications. "I believe Adam's out for revenge against us. He's not over what happened at the parsonage, and for him to be proven wrong about your guilt has him seeing red."

Elizabeth nodded her head. "I'll be testifying in a few minutes, and after that, Wayne is testifying. Adam can't trip us up, because we'll tell the truth. All we can do is pray for God to touch the hearts of the jury." She twirled her hair with her right forefinger. "I was watching their faces with Madeline's testimony. I believe they felt sorry for her. If they believe she did it in self-defense, they will come back with a verdict finding her innocent." Her blue eyes sparkled. "Then, she'll be able to have a new beginning."

Joe did a marvelous job of questioning Elizabeth and Wayne. It was quite clear that Adam was furious. He tried to trip them both up in his cross examinations but came off looking like he was trying to convict them. Luke saw some of the jurors shake their heads. "Boy, Joe, I think Adam needs to calm down. He's losing it."

Luke stroked his chin with his right thumb and forefinger. "Well, now it's up to the jury. May the Lord reveal Madeline was truly trying to defend herself."

Elizabeth gave a heavy sigh. "I think while the jury's out, we should get something to eat. I'm really hungry after all this."

Luke combed back his curls with his right hand. "I know what you mean. You seemed like a lamb before the wolves. It was quite marvelous the way you answered him. I'm sure the jury was rather confused at his badgering you that way. I watched their faces and expressions."

Wayne chimed in. "I know I'm starving. If you don't mind, I'll follow you to wherever you go."

Elizabeth smiled. "Wayne, I wish I'd known you better before. It'll be a pleasure to have you join us. As a matter of fact, after Luke and I are married, we'd appreciate if you and Jane could become our friends."

Wayne shook back tears. "I'm so grateful for your forgiveness." He grabbed her right hand between his hands. "Jane and I would consider it an honor to be friends with you and Luke." He laughed and nodded towards Luke. "That guy was supposed to be investigating Barth's murder, yet it was apparent he was more concerned in proving your innocence. He was your staunchest supporter."

Pastor O'Reilly interjected. "I know I didn't go through any of it personally, but I sure did in my spirit." He clasped his hands together. "I'm with Elizabeth. I'm extremely hungry after that battle."

Luke, Elizabeth, Joe, Wayne, and Pastor O'Reilly all walked into Margie's to find May, Nathan, Pete, and Connie there. May came over to them. "How'd it go?" She gestured with her right hand. "I thought it was quite ridiculous of Adam to limit entrance into the courtroom. But he's an angry man out for revenge."

Nathan interjected. "But we've been praying for him to find himself kicking against the pricks." He paused. "How did it go?"

Luke looked at Elizabeth. "It was as if he had Elizabeth on trial. I watched the jury, and I know they were confused at his tactics." He blew out a heavy sigh. "To be honest, if I was on the jury, I would have felt sorry for Madeline. It was apparent she was duped by the guy. Wayne made it clear she was nothing more than Barth's toy." He paused. "Elizabeth and Wayne's testimonies were incredible. There wasn't a person in the courtroom who doubted the character of Barth after their testimony. The more Adam tried to break them down, the stronger their testimony became."

Wayne piped in. "Madeline came off being the victim after her testimony."

Joe rubbed his temple with his left hand. "Her testimony really touched the heart. She's really become a changed woman. Extenuating circumstances from her childhood led her to turn from the Lord. A devastated child can make a lot of mistakes, but she sees it all now."

Margie came over to welcome them all. "I'm so pleased to see you all. If you take a seat, I'll bring out the day's specials. Is that acceptable with all of you?"

Pastor O'Reilly answered. "We'll all be quite pleased with your daily special"

They took seats, and Wayne asked Luke about the food. "How's the food here?"

"This diner used to belong to my sister, but she's getting married the same day as us." He gestured with his right hand towards May. "She's a great cook, but Margie's a master at it. It doesn't matter what she makes, it's always outstanding."

Wayne bit the hangnail on his right thumb. "Jane is a great woman, but she'll be the first to admit she lacks in the cooking arena. If it's that good, Jane and I may be moving to Burroughville." He shook his head. "We can't seem to find a reasonable place to eat in Capital City." His eyebrows scrunched together. "Is there a reasonable place for sale?"

Joe laughed. "It seems the previous Chief of Police has his house up for sale. You can be sure it's top of the line." He paused. "But it's quite expensive."

Elizabeth piped in. "Joe, buy it today for him. I'll take care of the expense." She blushed. "I mean, if it's all right with Luke?"

Luke chuckled. "It's fine with me. I believe God wants them to have a new beginning." He gazed at Wayne. "Will you and Jane accept our gift?"

Wayne choked up. "I'm so overwhelmed by the goodness of you two. My pension from the service is okay, but not having a mortgage will help." He grabbed Luke's hand with his hands. "I can't wait to tell Jane. She has felt the Lord prompting for some time to move out of the city, but she had no direction." He paused. "There's only one thing about us moving to Burroughville that we must know. Is there a descent Bible preaching church in town?"

Joe piped in. "You're talking to the assistant pastor of the local church." He pointed towards Pastor O'Reilly. "That man, along with Luke are two of the best Bible preachers I've ever heard."

Wayne gazed at Luke. "You didn't tell me you were a pastor."

Luke chuckled. "It's a long story."

Margie started to bring out their meals. Wayne stared. "It's corned beef and cabbage. I haven't had that since my mother died. She made a delicious corned beef and cabbage."

Luke grinned. "I'm sure she did, but Margie has a way of surpassing any other cooking."

Wayne took a bite and his jaw dropped. "I never thought anyone would surpass my mother's cooking. This is incredible." He paused. "I know where Jane and I'll be eating when we move here."

Joe interrupted. "Oh yes, Bob Hopkins and his wife left all their furniture. That's another reason the price is up there. The house includes an indoor pool, a tennis court, an oriental garden, and other amenities." He gestured with his right hand. "You see, his wife comes from money. They wanted to leave Burroughville behind them. As far as I know, they moved to France and only took their personal belongings. All else is still there. Whatever you don't want, you can donate to charity."

May came over to be officially introduced to Wayne. "I'm May Drake, and I've heard many good things about you. I hope we get the opportunity to get better acquainted."

May put out her right hand. "I'm so pleased to meet you." She reached over to take Nathan's right hand. "This is Nathan

O'Conner, my future husband." She paused. "Nathan, this is Wayne Olson, the one I told you about. He's the one who helped give Luke the evidence to clear Elizabeth."

Nathan took Wayne's right hand between his. "It's a pleasure to meet you. We knew Elizabeth was innocent, but the former chief was convinced of her guilt. Thank the good Lord Luke met you."

They had just finished eating when, Teresa, Joe's assistant came in. "Joe, the jury has reached a verdict. They need you back in court."

"Wow!" Joe said. "That was fast. I pray it's a good sign."

§

Joe, Luke, Elizabeth, Pastor O'Reilly, and Wayne hurried into the courtroom. Once the judge was seated, he turned towards the defendant. "Would the defendant please rise and face the jury?"

Madeline slowly rose, took a deep breath, and faced the jury. The judge then turned his attention towards them. "What is the verdict of the jury?"

"We find the defendant not guilty."

Madeline fell backwards into her chair.

The judge addressed the jury. "Thank you jury for your time. You are excused." He paused for the jury to leave. "Court is adjourned."

Joe threw up his hands. "Praise the Lord!"

Elizabeth and Luke hurried over to Madeline. Elizabeth hugged her. "I'm so pleased for you."

Madeline had tears pouring down her cheeks. "All I know is you're a tremendous person. I'm so sorry for what I thought of you. What Barth put you through, and he convinced me you were this wicked woman." She hung her head. "I don't know what I'm going to do now. I don't have an income or formal education."

Elizabeth took her right hand in hers. "If you could start over, have a new beginning, where would you go? I mean, if you were somewhat well off?"

Madeline's eyebrows scrunched together. "I think I'd like to fulfill my mother's dream of living in Hawaii. She had all sorts of pictures of Hawaii." She gestured with her right hand. "Apparently, her mother came from there and wished she could go back." She sighed. "It seems neither one of them were able to do it." Her eyebrows scrunched together. "Why do you ask?"

Luke gestured towards Elizabeth. "You see my future wife and I are going to fulfill your wish. We'll buy you a place on the main island and set you up with a substantial monthly income."

Elizabeth's blue eyes sparkled. "I believe we'll set you up, and then give you a third of what Barth was getting. That's about twenty-seven thousand dollars a month."

Madeline's eyes bulged. "A month!" She paused. "Are you saying Barth had a million dollars a year?"

"Yes."

Madeline hugged Elizabeth. "I wish I would've known you before." She hung her head. "But I think all that happened was needed. I had to come to myself like the Prodigal Son." Her brown eyes teared. "I was really rolling in the mire." Tears rolled down her cheeks. "But my Father was waiting with open arms for me to come home."

Elizabeth took her right hand. "You'll stay with me at the manor while we find you a place and get things taken care of." She paused. "Would you be willing to be a bridesmaid at our wedding?"

Madeline's jaw fell. "I can't think of a greater honor. It would make me quite happy."

"Okay. It's settled then." Elizabeth put her hair behind her ears with both hands. "Before you leave for Hawaii, I want to fit you out with all new clothes." She paused. "I have a feeling you'll want to give all your clothes to charity. If I'm correct, Barth purchased them. It's best if all traces of your past were out of your sight. Am I right?"

Madeline hung her head. "I would constantly remember they were purchased with your money. It would continually make me ashamed." She smiled. "Besides, I prayed for the Lord to help me replace them." She gestured with her right hand. "I don't believe much of them would be appropriate for someone who has been translated out of darkness into God's marvelous light."

Wayne interjected. "Well, the Lord has answered your prayers through these two." He gestured his right hand towards Luke and Elizabeth. "These two are setting up Jane and me here in Burroughville."

Luke reached into his right pants pocket, pulled out his keys, and handed them to Wayne. "I don't know if you'd like a Ferrari, but I'm not one for sports cars. Just give me a Mercedes. That's my idea of class." He paused. "I have the title in the car, Elizabeth will sign it over to you. Just let us know how much it'll be to register. The cost is on us." He gave a slow grin. "Well, it's really on Elizabeth."

Elizabeth giggled. "Luke and I seem to be of one mind. The Lord leads us to what has to be done."

Wayne's eyes bulged as he took the keys. "I always wanted to drive one of those, but I never thought I would." He gave a throaty laugh. "I do believe that Jane and I are moving on up to the Eastside."

They all laughed. While they were laughing, May and Nathan came in. May hugged Madeline. "We heard the jury found you innocent. We're so pleased."

Luke combed his black curls with his right hand. "It seems Elizabeth has a bridesmaid, but I need a groomsman." He grinned at Wayne. "Would you be so kind as to fill the position?"

"I would be proud and honored to be part of your wedding."

Joe picked up his briefcase. "I guess we'd better get out of here. Besides, I have to look into buying that house for Wayne." He paused. "Do you want me to see what can be done for Madeline in Hawaii?" He paused. "Teresa can handle it; she has some ties in Hawaii."

Luke nodded his head. "That would be perfect." He threw up his hands. "I don't know anything about Hawaii except that it's the fiftieth state."

Elizabeth giggled. "I guess that sums up what I know about Hawaii." She paused. "Please do let Teresa handle it."

Luke gave a puzzled look. "Joe, what would you and Carol like? We've been seeing to all of these, but I believe the Lord is saying there's a desire in the hearts of you and Carol." He paused. "What is it?"

Joe's mouth dropped. "We've always admired the Paxton Estate, and we heard Holly Paxton is selling. Since Marshall past away, she doesn't want to stay here any longer. She has a sister on the East Coast and wants to move back there." He rubbed his temple with the fingers of his left hand. "It's quite out of our league, but it is the desire of our hearts."

Elizabeth nodded towards Luke. "Joe, you just go and buy it at our expense." She paused. "Once it's purchased, will you be able to keep it up?"

Joe shook his head. "I do a pretty good business, but I don't know if it's enough to keep a place like that up."

"Would an extra ten thousand dollars a month be enough?" Elizabeth touched his right arm. "Joe, you've been an incredible help in all of this. If you need more, you let Luke and I know."

"I don't think I'll need more than that." He grabbed Luke's right hand. "Luke, I'm so grateful to the Lord for sending you to the parsonage that day. To think, I could've missed all this."

Elizabeth twirled her hair around her right forefinger. "Joe, I believe God wants us to have your office handle all our business. Samuel McIntyre, in Boston, is the one who handles it at present at the Powers, Farmington, Randall Law Firm. Matthew Powers is the owner, but I don't believe there'll be a problem getting Samuel here." She paused. "I'll purchase a partnership for him in your office. That way all our business will be handled here."

Luke grabbed his head with both hands. "That's a marvelous idea. This way we don't have to travel or contact Boston to handle anything." He paused. "But Joe, would you want a partner?"

Joe gave out a heavy sigh. "I was praying to the Lord about it. However, I didn't know anyone who could afford to be a partner. Teresa could, but she doesn't want to take on that much responsibility. She and her husband live a comfortable life. He owns the Simpson Department Stores. She only works because she loves the job." He paused. "Wow! Wait until I tell Carol." He laughed. "I'll have to tie her down to keep her from floating away."

Elizabeth's eyebrows scrunched together. "Oh yes, Joe do you know of any other estate for sale that would be suitable for your partner?"

Joe nodded. "This is incredible. Teresa told me the Appleton's Estate went up this morning. It's quite plush." He shook his head. "I believe Samuel would do quite nicely owning such a place."

"Praise God! I'll call him directly and explain what's going on. Then I'll get the necessary information from him. His wife's name is Deborah. She giggled. "The last time I saw him, he said they'd love to get out of the cold climate." She paused. "They're both Christians, I attend their church when I'm there." She touched Joes' right arm. "As soon as I get the information, could that be taken care of also?"

"I believe I'll take care of that."

Luke's face screwed up. "Wayne, how much is your pension?"

"I get twenty-eight hundred dollars a month from the service." He paused. "Jane makes about twenty-five hundred a month as a dental assistant.

Elizabeth shook her head. "That'll not do. You'll now receive an extra twenty thousand dollars a month." She put her hair behind her ears with both hands. "I believe that should keep you on the Eastside."

Everyone laughed.

Joe gave Luke a hug. "God truly has a call on your life. Carol and I have never uttered a word about this to anyone. Only God knew our heart's desire." He gestured with his left hand. "I do believe it's a new beginning for us too." He paused. "I'll see you all later, I have a lot to get done. I'll handle the situation for Wayne. When you get Samuel's information, I'll handle that. In the meantime, I'll give an offer in their name." He threw up his hands. "I'll tell Carol and get Teresa to see to the Paxton Estate directly. Then she'll see about the Hawaii situation for Madeline. If things go well, it should only be a matter of a couple of days for everything." He laughed. "When you're dealing with cash, things go quite smoothly."

Luke looked at Wayne. "Do you think I can borrow your car until I get something else?"

Wayne laughed. "It's ten years old, you can have it. When you're finished, you can donate it to someone in need." He paused, took out his keys, and handed them to Luke. "Be my guest." He gave a slow grin. "I now drive a Ferrari."

Elizabeth turned towards Madeline. "I think we should leave. Is there anything you want to keep from your apartment?"

"Yes. I have some things of my mother." She gestured with her right hand. "Just pictures and a few small mementos." Her eyes filled with tears. "My mother was a God-fearing woman who lived for the Lord. I was so angry at God for taking her, that I didn't see her suffering was over. The cancer was awful, but she never stopped praising the Lord."

Elizabeth gave her a hug. "I know the pain of losing parents. I lost mine at an early age. My grandmother raised me, but she died right after I received my inheritance." She paused. "It was in my grief that I met Barth." She threw up her hands. "The rest is history. Thank the Lord I'm forgiven for marrying a non-believer. I'm just so thankful."

Wayne joined in. "I know I am." He laughed. "Wait until I tell Jane, she's going to be ecstatic." He paused. "I do believe it's time for her to quit work and enjoy our new home."

Chapter 15

One Can Make A Difference

May and Nathan left right after the wedding for Europe. Nathan had some business needing immediate attention.

Luke and Elizabeth sat at Margie's Diner for the lunch special, when Wayne and Jane came in. Jane hugged Elizabeth. "I'm so pleased to have you for a friend. It's been difficult finding someone with like-minded faith." She gestured towards Luke. "You both have brightened up our lives. We love fellowshipping with you." She grabbed Elizbeth's right hand. "I can't express my excitement with words. It's such a pleasure to stay home and take care of our beautiful place."

Margie came over and placed her hands on her hips. "I suppose you're all here for my lunch special. Today is lasagna, spinach salad, garlic bread, and banana cream pie."

Luke gave a slow smile. "That sounds delicious. My palate can already savor the flavors." He chuckled. "After all, I've enjoyed all this before at your house."

"Outside of Mitchell, you seem to be my best fan."

Elizabeth interjected. "Well, he's telling the truth about your cooking. I wish we could find someone who cooks like you to work for us at Drake Manor." She paused. "It's quite shameful when we have to come here to get a great meal." She put her hair behind her ears with both hands. "We'd really love to have meals like this at home."

Luke nodded. "It would be great to have dinner parties at home with our friends."

"Really? I think I may be able to help. My cousin, Mabel Truman, on the West Coast has recently become widowed. She's barely getting by." She paused. "It seems all their savings went on hospital bills. She's only forty-five. They never had any children, so I'm the only family she has left." She laughed. "What I'm trying to say is that Mabel can cook better than me. She's the one who taught me. I have the gift, but she has an even greater gift."

Luke interjected. "Wow! If she can cook better than you, that's almost unbelievable."

Elizabeth gave a slow grin. "Do you think Mabel would be willing to come and be our cook?"

Margie grabbed Elizabeth's right hand. "She'd love it." She paused. "She's coming here in two days to live with Mitchell and me. However, I know she'd much rather cook at the manor. Especially with the dinner parties you'll both have. She'll be thrilled." She gave a heavy sigh. "I better get everyone their lunch. After the rush, I'll call Mabel and tell her."

While Margie went to get their lunch specials, Joe and Carol came in. When Joe saw Luke and Elizabeth, his face lit up. "Luke, I can't express my gratitude for your faithfulness to the Lord. If I didn't allow the Holy Spirit to work in my heart, I would have joined Adam and Janice in leaving the church." He threw up his hands. "Thank God for the difference you made in our lives with speaking truth."

Carol gave Elizabeth a hug. "I'm so sorry for not getting to know you before." She gestured towards her husband. "We had become part of the blind leading the blind. But as Paul on the road to Damascus, the scales fell from our eyes when Luke said what he did at the parsonage." Her eyes filled with tears. "You two are examples of what a Christian should be. I can't thank God enough for opening our eyes to see what we had become."

Joe interjected. "You both have no idea what moving into that house felt like. It was as if we moved into a dream." He gestured with his left hand. "But it's a reality God made possible through the kindness and love of you two."

Luke gave a slow grin. "Yes, but it was God and not us. If he hadn't blessed us, we couldn't be a blessing to anyone else."

Joe grabbed Luke's right hand between his. "True, but you both had to be willing to do it."

Elizabeth giggled. "Okay. Enough of this. We all thank God for his love, mercy, and blessings."

Everyone said. "Amen!"

Joe gestured with his left hand. "Not to change the subject, but how did Madeline make out?"

Luke chuckled. "She's one grateful woman to the Lord. When she left, she asked if Elizabeth and I would visit her." He paused. "We told her it would be easier for her to visit us."

Carol's eyes filled with tears. "I was so pleased at what the Lord did for her." She gave a heavy sigh. "Like I said at the parsonage, I almost killed someone. Mine wouldn't have been self-defense. My selfish pride would have done it." She paused. "I'll be glad to get to know her when she visits here."

While they were talking, Pastor O'Reilly came in. "Did I walk into a fellowship meeting?"

Luke chuckled. "It sure seems like it." He paused. "Margie just told us her cousin, Mabel, cooks better than her. Praise the Lord! She'll be here in two days as our cook at the manor. Now, we'll be able to invite people to eat at our house." He grabbed his head with both hands. "What a difference having her will make."

Elizabeth twirled her hair around her right forefinger. "There's something else I feel strongly about concerning our staff." She gave a heavy sigh. "It's Harold and Sarah Simpson."

Before she could finish, Luke interjected. "They're getting up in years. It's time they retired and had life easier." He paused. "I know they're from Northern Ireland. Perhaps, they'd like to retire there in a nice house with a substantial income?"

"Exactly!" Elizabeth said. "They've mentioned several times how they miss Ireland, but didn't want to leave me." She giggled. "We'll see if someone from Joe's office can go there with them, help them find what they want, and handle the sale. Then we'll give them an income sufficient for them to have servants to wait on them for the rest of their life."

Joe nodded. "I believe Teresa and her husband, James, will do it." He laughed. "James has family in Ireland, and they were going to spend next month there." He paused. "I'll tell her directly and get reservations for the Simpsons."

"Praise God! They'll be the lord and lady of their manor." Luke's face screwed up. "Who'll take their places in the house? They do run things."

Elizabeth's eyes filled with tears. "I'll sorely miss them. They've been like adopted parents to me. I love them both very much, and I want to make the rest of their lives comfortable." She paused. "We'll definitely have to visit them." She put her hair back behind her ears with both hands. "I think Tom and Susan Jeffers can take their places quite easily." She paused. "I believe we'll stop at the Manor before we tend to our business, have Tom and Susan move into to the Simpson's quarters, have them move Harold and Sarah into the best guest room, and they'll take over Harold and Sarah's duties today. If they have any questions, Harold and Sarah will have two weeks to help them before leaving." Her eyebrows scrunched together. "There's this couple at church I've noticed for some time. I believe their names are Jacob and Anna Salisbury. They appear to be in their forties and have no children. I wonder if they'd be willing to take Tom and Susan's place?"

Pastor O'Reilly clasped his hands. "That's the Lord's doing. They've been struggling for some time financially. Last year, they lost their house and haven't been able to find a decent job." He paused. "I don't know if you noticed one of the Sunday School classes is locked. I've allowed them to stay there. They buy their food and use the kitchen. Both are incredibly clean. If I didn't know they used the kitchen, I would find no traces of it." He grabbed Luke's right hand with both his hands. "They told me God promised their deliverance was on its way." He laughed. "They'll be more than happy to be your chauffeur and housekeeper, receive a salary, and free lodgings."

"I know who they are," Luke said, "and they're always so attentive to your messages. It's obvious they love the Lord." He paused. "Would you tell them to meet us here at six for supper?"

Pastor O'Reilly clasped his hands. "They'll be here and waiting for you."

As they were eating, Pete and Connie came in. Pete laughed when he saw the others. "I do believe Margie's has become the place of fellowship for Burroughville Christian Fellowship Church." He looked at what everyone was eating. "Lasagna! It looks like we chose the right day to come." He laughed. "Of course, I had no choice, it's my day off."

Luke stroked his chin with his right thumb and forefinger. "How are you two doing?"

"We're all settled into our home," Connie said. "It's so nice. We're beside ourselves every time we pull up to it and see our name on the mailbox."

Luke and Elizabeth gazed at each other and nodded. "Elizabeth and I have been so busy, we haven't had a chance to check up on you." He combed back his curls with his right hand. You'll need a new car to pull up to your new home." He paused. "And I do believe your income has increased an extra ten-thousand dollars a month."

Pete's mouth fell open. "Oh my! This is too much. I mean, you paid off our debts, gave us your beautiful home, and now this." He gave a throaty laugh. "Although we love pulling up to the house, we felt a new car would be the cherry on the cake." He grabbed Luke's right hand with his hands. "Thank you, thank you, and thank you. You two are definitely the Lord's vessels unto good works that give glory to him."

Luke chuckled. "Well, what's your heart's desire for a vehicle? We really do have to hurry to take care of some things and be back here for supper. Jacob and Anna will be waiting for us, and we don't want them to think we stood them up."

Pete looked at Connie, and she shook her head. "Well, Connie and I both thought if we could choose our heart's desire, we would choose a Mercedes SUV." He scratched the back of his head with his right hand. "Of course, we were pipe dreaming."

Elizabeth smiled. "Well, let's get your pipe dream. Thank God, the dealership is close by." She paused. "We'll take you there. Then Luke and I'll talk to the manager, and we'll leave you a signed check. You pick out your dream vehicle and make sure you have all the necessary warranties. You just fill in the amount of the check."

"If you're free for supper," Luke said, "you can meet us here." He put up his right hand. "Please don't be intimidated by any price tag. You must get the one your heart desires."

§

Elizabeth was beside herself with joy. "Luke, I had all I could do to take care of our business after dropping Pete and Connie off at Mercedes of Burroughville. I felt as if I was getting a Christmas present to see their elation." She paused. "Then to tell Tom and Susan they'd be our new butler and housekeeper. Their faces lit up like Christmas trees." She giggled. "But the greatest was when we told Harold and Sarah what we planned for them." Her eyes teared. "I was overjoyed at their elation. I believe their excitement caused them to appear twenty years younger." She paused. "Praise the Lord I'm no longer out of his will in an unequal yoke. It was a long and difficult trial, but I just kept pressing forward in the faith."

"I know what you mean. After the Lord laid on my heart that I'd make a difference in this town, I encountered storms and obstacles one after another. Faith encouraged me to keep pressing forward, and I'd reap in his season." He gestured with his right hand. "When he says one can make a difference, he'll work through the person to bring about his will."

"He's so awesome."

Luke nodded his head. "Amen!" He chuckled. "But I had no idea it would be this fantastic." He reached over and touched her left arm. "To be given you was more than I could've ever dreamed. But to be wealthy and the means to bless others is just amazing."

Elizabeth's eyes teared. "I can't describe my elation at being the Lord's hands to bless others." She paused. "Before I inherited my fortune, I heard a sermon based on the parable of the rich fool who built bigger barns. The Lord impressed me he doesn't bless us to hoard our money, but to bless his children." She reached over and touched Luke's right arm. "Because the heart of God desires to bless his children, it fulfills us when we do the blessing."

"Praise the Lord he didn't have us take a honeymoon. What we've been doing is far more rewarding than travelling around old buildings."

Elizabeth giggled. "I wholeheartedly agree. I'm just overjoyed at seeing the faces of those who are blessed."

Luke chuckled. "Well, it looks like we're at Margie's. Let's see Jacob and Anna and do some more blessing."